I0640180

DiamondVania

Eric Hua

Published by Eric Hua, 2025.

DIAMONDVANIA

First edition. May 8, 2025.

ISBN: 978-1069406828

Written by Eric Hua.

Table of Contents

This book is written for my students of the 2024/2025 school year.

Thank you to my editor Pam!

Prologue

It was a dark night with clouds scattered through the sky in the town of Diamondvania. An angry mob was gathering with their torches and pitchforks at hand. They were all making their way away from the town and into the forest. A house hidden within the woods was located outside the town square.

Inside was a man who was reading through the pages of his book. He had drawn a magical circle on the ground as shown in his book's diagram. Beside the circle were candles meticulously placed around. He made sure to carefully light up each candle and when the task was done, he was ready to perform the ritual.

He referred to his book when suddenly, he heard a knock on his door.

"Bal? Open up! We know you're in there!"

It was the angry villagers knocking on his door. He knew this day would come, but wasn't expecting it to be so soon. He frantically flipped through the book's pages, hoping to skip through the needless instructions and right to the incantation.

"HE'S NOT OPENING THE door." One of the villagers said.

"What are we going to do?" The mob of people were talking amongst themselves when another of them spoke up.

"Step aside. I'm breaking the door down!" He said while holding his axe.

THE MAN INSIDE CONTINUED flipping through the pages. "Come on, where is it?" He said to himself. The pages moved faster and faster and then it stopped. "Found it!" He read through the spell and stood by the circle, reciting everything he had read.

"What? Why did nothing happen?"

He was confused but had no time to investigate further as he heard the front door break into the room. The villagers rammed through the door with their torches and pitchforks in hand. They searched the main floor and the upper room but they saw no one. Many were ready to give up until one of them stumbled through a hidden door.

It led to a dark basement that gave off an ominous aura. The villagers carefully descended the stairs and when they arrived, they were appalled by what they saw.

"What dark sorcery is this?" A shocked villager yelped.

"He has been practicing the forbidden arts." Another one claimed.

"He must be dealt with immediately!" The third one demanded.

"Where is he now?"

The villagers that were in the basement began looking around but they could not find him. While they were distracted, Bal snuck up the stairs quietly and slipped through the entrance. He would have made a clean escape but he stepped on some branches, which alerted some of the villagers.

"HE'S ESCAPING!"

"AFTER HIM!"

Bal ran through the dark forest looking behind him nervously. He could see the light from their torches and hear their angry voices. He was about to pick up the pace, but when he turned to face forward, he immediately stopped as he was met with a cliff. It was a long way down from where he stood, about a twenty-foot drop. He was going to turn around but the angry mob with their pitchforks were looming.

"Drop the book, Bal. You can still turn back. Just surrender yourself and leave the book to us." One of the people in the crowd tried to reason with him.

Bal looked down at the cliff, then at the mob before him, and finally his book. A couple of men tried to apprehend him while he was still thinking, but Bal had made his decision. Instead of staying still, he leaned back and let himself descend off the cliff.

Some of the members of the crowd gathered at the edge and although it was dark, they heard the sound of a body hitting the ground. They all pitied the man and gave him a moment of silence.

Shortly after, rain began to pour down from the sky. The weather had doused their anger and their torches. Then they slowly returned to the town.

Meanwhile in the basement, where Bal failed to perform the ritual. The magical circle began to glow as dark energy began to flow out of it. Whatever it was Bal was trying to do, he had succeeded but that was only the start. A terrible darkness was about to fall on Diamondvania.

Chapter 1: Holy Templar

Away from Diamondvania, was a large temple up in the highlands. Inside were young aspiring initiates training to become templars.

Templars were high-ranking holy warriors who had garnered much respect through their intense training. These trials included: martial arts, meditation, and a mission beyond the walls of the temple. Only those who have mastered those skills and accomplished their quest could attain such status.

There was one such warrior amid her journey. She had defeated all her peers in combat training and was about to leave to rest for the day.

"Afomia, wait up!"

"Sifu Ruthar! She bowed to pay her respect to her teacher.

"Oh, there is no need for that. Get up!"

"So what's the rush?"

"Trying to play it cool I see. Well, there is no need to hide it. Everyone already knows." Ruthar said, raising his eyebrows.

"About what?" Afomia was legitimately confused.

"That you are the top fighter among all the initiates! If you keep this up, you might prove to be even better than your older brother."

"Oh, but I can't take all the credit. You trained me after all."

"Well, I am a pretty good teacher if I do say so myself!" Ruthar chuckled.

"Thank you for coming all this way to congratulate me." Afomia beamed.

"Oh, I didn't rush over here just to compliment you."

"There's more?" The girl wondered.

"Yes, there have been strange occurrences happening in the city of Diamondvania. Many humans and livestock have been disappearing at an alarming rate."

"What was the cause?"

"Unknown. That is why I'm here to ask you to investigate. Consider this as your mission." Afomia's Sifu said matter of factly.

"So if I succeed in alleviating Diamondvania's problem, will I become a templar?"

"Well, yes, but..." Sifu Ruthar started but was cut off.

"Alright, I will take it!" Afomia exclaimed.

"Afomia, I know you are excited about this opportunity to realize your dream but, please listen to my words."

"My apologies Sifu Ruthar. I got carried away. Please continue."

"If this mission proves to be more dangerous than you initially anticipated, I urge you to not proceed. Return at once, and report back to the Templars. Understood?"

"Yes, Sifu Ruthar. You have my word."

"Good. Well then, you better get some rest. You have a long journey ahead."

"Try not to miss me too much." Afomia teased. As she was leaving, she felt a small pebble hit her back. "Hey!" She called out as she turned around.

"Don't worry. I never miss!" Sifu Ruthar said as he ran away.

Chapter 2: The Hunter

I t was late morning in Diamondvania. The streets were filled with people despite everything that had happened in this city. Music could be heard playing in the marketplace, where vendors were open for business like any other regular day. However, on this particular day, there was going to be a unique visitor within the town.

"Step right up everybody!" A vendor was trying to get everyone's attention. "Would anyone like the chance to win 50 silver coins?"

Upon hearing his announcement, a large crowd formed around the shop.

"Oh my, we have an eager audience today. That's what I like to see! Well, let me explain the rules!"

He placed an apple on a wooden stand and moved about fifteen feet away to mark a horizontal line. "For the price of one silver coin, you must land a perfect hit on that apple with this dagger. Oh, and you have to stand behind this line."

Many raised a silver coin with their hand, wanting the opportunity to claim the prize. "Well then, I bid you all, good luck!"

The merchant received the people's money one by one, and each contestant took to their spot and threw the dagger at the apple. Many tried but none succeeded. Some were close but the dagger would always get repelled away, leaving the apple unscathed. In fact, there was one throw that seemed like a bullseye but at the last moment, however, it bounced off.

"Oh! So close, but no cut on the apple, so no prize for you!"

After seeing that attempt, the villagers became discouraged.

"Is there no one else willing to take on this challenge?!" Despite how much profit he already made, the vendor wanted more. He looked around, and not seeing any other takers, was about to call off the challenge.

"I'll go." A young man with glasses and a cloth raised his hand.

"Oh, a new contestant. Very well, step right up!"

"Wait, how about we make this a little more interesting?" The young man asked.

"I'm listening." The older man responded.

"I will wage ten silver coins but I get to choose my weapon."

The vendor inspected an arrow that the man said he would use. It was made of wood. The merchant's greed crept into his smile, but he tried his best to hide it. He looked at the young man and asked.

"This is your weapon of choice?"

"It is indeed."

"Deal!"

The contestant stood behind the line and pulled out his bow to aim the wooden arrow. He released the shot and the vendor was anticipating a hefty profit with this gamble. That was until he saw the wooden arrow pierce through the apple.

"What? There is no way! He must have cheat..."

Before he could finish, the marksman fired two more wooden arrows that also hit the target. The merchant went silent but the crowd was in awe. The man took the bag and threw it in the air. The silver coins scattered in the sky and began raining down on the town. All the villagers scrambled to get as much money as they could. In contrast, the peddler was in shambles, grieving over all his lost money.

As the bowman was about to leave the town square, he bumped into the mayor of Diamondvania.

"Well done! What a show you put on Mister...?"

"Ehsaas. Just call me Ehsaas."

"Very well! Ehsaas it is!"

"I'm guessing you are the mayor who called for my services?" The Archer guessed.

"Ah yes, that is me, Mayor Corrin! You must tell me, how were you able to beat that vendor's game? It seemed like he had everyone fooled."

"Oh, it was quite simple. There was an anti-magnet hidden within the apple. Any metal that gets near such a thing, would be repelled away instantly. That's why the vendor chose those metal daggers. The daggers could never put a dent in the apple."

"Wow, that is quite clever."

"You are too kind Mayor Corrin. So what do you require my help with?" Ehsaas asked.

"Come to my office, this is no place to speak about such matters."

Ehsaas followed the mayor to a building close to the entrance of the town. There was nothing extravagant about the room, but there were many papers all over Mayor Corrin's desk.

"You seem to be quite the busy man." Ehsaas noticed.

"Oh, let me tell you, running a town is no laughing matter." The Mayor replied.

"I don't think I could ever handle such responsibilities."

"Nonsense. If you can hunt creatures out in the woods, then being mayor should be no problem for you!"

"So what kind of creature will I be asked to take down for you today?"

"Actually, we aren't sure ourselves. There have been reports of many civilians disappearing." He handed some papers over to Eshaas who began studying them. "Every single one of these victims were attacked by a mysterious creature. Some have gone missing, but none that returned have any recollection of what the beast looked like."

Ehsaas couldn't find any clues at first glance, but he was not the kind to give up so easily. He looked back to the Mayor, letting him speak.

"I know this task is quite dangerous, but could you please put an end to this?"

"You can count on me. Hunter Ehsaas will take down your mysterious creature problem in no time!"

Chapter 3: The Summoner

Out in the forest during the night, a teenage girl who lived in the woods was wandering the area. Not wanting to be alone, she threw a stone with strange markings on it. Out of the stone emerged her companion: a spirit wolf. Together they walked through the forest, but after some time, the wolf picked up an unusual scent.

"What's wrong Saanvi?" The girl asked.

Her wolf companion then ran off, expecting her to follow. The young woman was caught by surprise, but she trusted her loyal companion and followed closely behind. The closer they got towards the scent, the slower and more cautious they became. When they noticed a small glimmer of light, the Summoner signalled for her companion to stay silent and remain near her, as they hid behind a rock.

In an open part of the woods, near a pond, there was a couple sitting together. As they were sharing romantic looks and exchanging sweet words, they continued to look up into a beautiful star-filled sky with a shining moon.

The animal wildspeaker was not interested in the couples' activity and was about to turn away. However, as she was about to leave, her companion suddenly became aggressive, growling in the couple's direction.

"Hey girl, that's enough. Calm..." She stopped mid-sentence as her attention was drawn to the woman screaming.

"AHHHHH!"

The male counterpart was going through a metamorphosis. His body increased in size and thick fur grew throughout his body. His nails turned into claws, and his face was completely distorted. He stood tall and howled towards the moon.

The woman was in such a state of shock that her legs were paralyzed. She hoped her once beloved boyfriend would remember her, but the gaze in his eyes was not human. He had lost his sense of reason and slashed at the defenseless woman but Saanvi hopped on the werewolf's back.

With the beast distracted, the Summoner appeared to help the woman.

"Are you alright?"

"Who are you? What is that thing?! Where is my boyfriend?!"

"My name is Olivia and that thing over there is..."

She stopped when she saw Saanvi thrown on the ground just a few meters from her. Both women looked at the werewolf that was approaching them. Finally, the fearful lady realized what was going on but refused to believe it. She tried to call out her boyfriend's name, hoping he would respond to her but in contrast, it returned a fierce howl. Olivia covered her ears but the woman beside her, fainted.

Seeing one of the humans fall unconscious, the werewolf was about to approach its victim but Saanvi stood up between the beast and the women despite suffering a nasty limp on one of her legs. The werewolf grew overconfident, thinking its foe had already lost. That was until Olivia began weaving her hands and arms, leaving the attacker confused.

A light green glow appeared around her hands and the healing energy transferred over to her loyal companion. Saanvi was rejuvenated, which caused the opposing enemy to take a step back. Sensing its fear, Saanvi pounced straight for her enemy. The werewolf attempted to slash its oncoming foe, but Saanvi disappeared from its sight.

Olivia casted a speed enhancement spell, causing the enemy to lose track of its target. Olivia's ally reappeared above the werewolf and

Olivia followed up by invoking an empowering ability on Saanvi. With their combined effort, the werewolf took a critical hit from Saanvi's claw attack and fell to the ground.

After their victory, Olivia recalled her companion into the summoning stone. As she did so, the defeated beast reverted back to its human form. Seeing the unconscious couple, Olivia knew she couldn't just leave them alone. She pulled out a different stone and summoned another creature to her aid. This creature was much larger than the silver wolf and was able to carry the two humans.

Once they were safely secured on the animal's back, Olivia called for her new companion to make its way to Diamondvania.

Chapter 4: The Magician

On the next morning in Diamondvania, Ehsaas could hear a loud noise outside. He was staying at an inn that was provided to him by the mayor. Not wanting to be disturbed, he closed the windows and blinds, before returning to his investigation.

MEANWHILE, IN THE CITY square, a crowd had formed as an unconscious couple had been left on the ground. The townspeople were murmuring over what they should do. No one wanted to take initiative until Mayor Corrin appeared.

He assessed the female victim first and determined that she required medical attention. Two women from the crowd volunteered to help take the lady to the doctor. That left the unconscious male but before the mayor had the chance to check his vitals, tha man woke up. The crowd let out a sigh of relief.

"Ugh, where am I?" The man croaked.

"Easy there. You have been brought back to the town. Do you remember anything?" The Mayor asked while checking the man's condition.

"I was with my girlfriend and we were attacked. Hey, where is she?"

"Relax, she is taken care of. Tell us what or who attacked you."

"I'm not sure, it's all a blur..." He held his head.

Suddenly someone called out from the crowd. "It was her!"

A man in the crowd accused a teenage girl who wore a dark-colored robe along with a cloak. It was clear she didn't want to draw attention to herself based on her outfit, but now it was too late.

"Everyone calm down, let's not be rash and make false accusations." The Mayor attempted to keep the peace.

"That girl is a witch!" The crowd let out a gasp and moved away from the girl. Murmurs also began to spread, as the man continued. "I've seen her sneaking around performing her foul sorcery when she thinks no one is watching!"

Anxiety and fear began to swirl amongst the crowd. They were about to approach the woman with hostile intent, but Mayor Corrin stepped in.

"Everyone stand down!" He then turned to speak hoping to douse the tension. "I have gotten to know many of you and have found all of you to be astounding citizens. Saanjh here is no different. She would never hurt anyone!"

"But if she is a witch, then none of us will be safe!" Another in the crowd shouted.

Everyone was growing restless and Saanjh, the Magician, had reached her limit so she finally decided to take initiative.

"That's enough!" As she let out her frustration, a huge stream of fire from the palm of her hand that randomly fizzled out in the air. The crowd was stunned by what they had just witnessed, and they were now quietly waiting for the mage to speak.

"My name is Saanjh and yes, I'm capable of performing magical arts. However, I did nothing to that man or his girlfriend."

"Everyone was filled with mixed emotions until one of the men yelled again. "She's lying! Magician or Witch, it does not matter! They are all the same; full of lies!"

Again, the villagers were enraged and turning into an angry mob. Saanjh looked around hoping for a way out but she was surrounded. She was hoping she wouldn't have to resort to using her powers however, it appeared she didn't have much choice. As she was about to cast a spell, someone took the crowd's attention.

Slamming her spear on the ground was the holy Templar, who had been watching everything. The people became silent in her presence as she continued making her way towards Saanjh. When she was about a meter away, she told the magician to stay still. Surprisingly, the mage complied.

The Templar closed her eyes and began motioning her hands. She then finished her sequence by pointing two fingers on her right hand at the nervous mage. A bright stream of light energy shot out of her fingers and struck Saanjh.

"How do you feel?" The Templar asked.

"Uh, I don't feel any different."

The female Knight smiled and turned around to speak, "She is telling the truth."

A majority of the audience accepted the Templar's words but there were a few skeptics.

"Hold on, how can we trust you? We don't even know what you were doing with all your silly hand gestures." One doubter questioned.

"I just performed a holy purification chant. If this mage was lying, she wouldn't be able to talk right now."

"Oh yes! I have heard the noble templars are capable of such a skill!" Mayor Corrin's statement gave further assurance to the people of Diamondvania.

Seeing no other reason to cause a commotion, the crowd started to slowly disperse. The man who was unconscious earlier was helped by some of the other villagers to guide him back home. Mayor Corrin thanked the Templar and apologized to Saanjh before leaving as he had other matters to attend to. That left only the two ladies in the town square.

"Thanks for having my back there." Saanjh expressed her gratitude.

"No worries. We outcasts need to stick together." The Templar smiled.

"What's your name and what brings you to this dreadful place?" The Mage asked.

"My name is Afomia. I've been sent here by my mentor to investigate the strange disappearances happening here in Diamondvania."

"Wow, you are quite brave. Or incredibly foolish."

"Very funny. So, I take it your name is Saanjh?"

"The one and only! Well, it was nice meeting you, but if you got nothing else, I'm going to head home and..."

"Wait, you said earlier you weren't the one responsible for attacking that man."

"What about it?" The Mage nodded.

"Then do you know who is?" TheTemplar pressed.

"Listen, you really shouldn't get too involved with this place. It's nothing but trouble." Saanjh could hear her tone change into a warning one and she wanted to leave but Afomia persisted.

"Please tell me. This mission is very important, and I can't return without completing it."

Saanjh saw the determination in Afomia's eyes, "Sigh, I guess owe you one for helping me back there. Follow me."

Chapter 5: Investigation

Despite all the commotion outside, Ehsaas was studying all the information that had been given to him by the mayor. Most of the files he was going through contained information of the people who went missing in Diamondvania. He was trying to locate commonalities between the missing victims: height, ethnicity, family lineage, but he found nothing.

He threw the papers down lightly, feeling a bit frustrated. This was going to be more difficult than his usual cases. As he was trying to relax, he heard a knock on the door. He went to answer and upon opening, he was met with one of Mayor Corrin's assistants.

"Good afternoon sir, my name is Elliot, and the mayor has sent me to ask if you require assistance with anything?"

"Oh no, I will be fine." Ehsaas replied.

"Are you sure? Food? Something to drink?" Elliot asked.

"Oh, I can't say no to free food." The Detective thought out loud.

"Very well Mr. Ehsaas, I shall return in a few minutes."

As the mayor's assistant turned away, Ehsaas noticed something on the assistant's hand. "Hey Elliot? What happened there?"

"Oh, I'm a bit clumsy. Accidentally got this small cut on my finger while working in the kitchen."

"Cut? Cut. Cut..." He had an epiphany. "Thank you!"

He slammed the door on Elliot who was confused. The Assistant shrugged his shoulders and went on his way.

Meanwhile, Ehsaas scrambled through the documents looking for the photos. He was focusing on all the injury reports.

"Slash on the arm. This one on the leg."

He spoke out loud to himself and he found a pattern: all the injuries were claw marks. Once he made that connection, he bolted out the door and ran past all the other rooms in the inn, then down the stairs. He looked around and located the kitchen where he found Elliot along with the cooking staff.

"Oh Mr. Ehsaas, your food isn't ready yet."

"I'm not here for that. Tell me, is there a place that contains the history of Diamondvania?"

"Hmm, I'm not certain, but your best bet would be the library."

"Where is that?" Ehsaas asked urgently.

"A few blocks down west."

"Thanks Elliot!" The Detective dashed out, not hearing Elliot's response.

"But Detective, your food. Sigh..." the Assistant was feeling defeated, but one of the chefs in the kitchen got curious.

"Elliot! Why the long face?"

"Oh, hey, Chef Lycan. You can cancel the food order. Our guest just ran off."

"Oh? Where is he going in such a rush?"

"The Library." Elliot shrugged.

"Very interesting..." The Chef mumbled to himself.

"Uh, Chef Lycan? Everything okay?"

"My apologies. I'm not feeling so well. Could I leave a bit earlier tonight?"

"I guess it's not too busy tonight. Alright, take the rest of the night off. I hope you feel better by tomorrow!" Elliot said, looking at the schedule.

"Thank you. I should be good by tomorrow."

Chef Lycan pretended to be sick until he left the kitchen. Once he was out of sight, he dropped the act and made his way towards the library.

OUT IN THE FOREST, Olivia had found a spot where she could have dinner. She was accompanied by her many animal companions. Together, they were enjoying their meals until the animals sensed something foul in the air.

They were all barking, roaring, cawing, or howling. Olivia was confused as to what could be causing her friends to be in such duress. She tried everything but nothing would calm them down. Wanting to get to the bottom of the ruckus, she recalled her summons to her stones, all except the eagle.

"Alright Max, lead the way." she said.

Her eagle began flying towards Diamondvania. Olivia raced through the forest, following her airborne critter that soared through the sky.

Chapter 6: The Abandoned Cabin

J ust outside the village, Afomia was following Saanjh's lead. The unfamiliarity of the area combined with the dark atmosphere would cause many to be frightened, but not Afomia. Instead, she was curious as to where the mage was leading her.

"Where are we going?" she asked Saanjh.

"Scared already? You can always turn back." The Enchanter suggested.

"A templar never runs away!" Afomia stated passionately.

"Alright, sheesh, calm down! I'm just messing with you. There's an abandoned cabin out here."

"Who would choose to live out in these parts of the woods?" The Templar questioned.

"Rumour has it that a mage practiced dark magic out here."

"You know the person?"

"No, but whatever he did, it really gives other mages like me a bad reputation! I need to get to the bottom of this and clear my name!"

Afomia was starting to understand Saanjh's motives. "So, you've been to this place many times before?"

"Just the outside. I've never been inside."

"And why is that?"

"Are you crazy? Me going into a spooky abandoned cabin in the middle of nowhere by my lonely self? Have you never read any night time horror stories!?"

"No. The Monastery is filled with stories but we are forbidden to bring dark tales within our walls."

"Wow. You live a pretty sheltered life."

Suddenly, they heard a noise which made Afomia react. She was ready to pull out her weapon, but it was just a couple of bats that flew from the trees. She looked to where the bats were flying from and saw the abandoned cabin nearby.

"We're here." Saanjh continued to lead them until they were at the front entrance. "I know I said this place is abandoned, but who knows what could have crawled into a place like this. We should be careful and..."

Immediately, Afomia kicked down the door to Saanjh's dismay.

"What are you doing?!" Saanjh exclaimed.

"I'm getting us inside." Afomia replied.

"Do you not know what it means to be cautious?"

"I am cautious. If anything were to attack us after I kicked down the door, I can take care of it with my spear."

Saanjh couldn't believe what she was hearing. However, after not hearing any other noises or seeing anything attack them, Afomia decided it was safe to enter. Not wanting to be left alone, Saanjh quickly followed after, holding a lantern in her hand.

Inside the place was a dining room, kitchen, bedroom and a living room. Although the furniture was all dusty and filled with cobwebs, nothing seemed out of the ordinary.

"Well this place has been a let down!" Saanjh exclaimed.

"Maybe..." Afomia was convinced there was more to this place than meets the eye.

"You found something?"

"No, but I can sense an eerie presence. It's faint but something unnatural has been here."

Saanjh began to lean against the wall. "Well, whatever that is, I hope we never..."

Suddenly, Saanjh fell through the wall and down a hidden staircase. Afomia ran to where Saanjh fell from and called to her. "Saanjh!"

"Oww, I'm okay. In pain, but okay." The Mage replied why rubbing her back.

Afomia let out a sigh of relief and walked down the flight of stairs. She then helped Saanjh back up, who picked up the lantern. They saw a path and continued down the hidden basement. When they hit the end, they found a room with partially melted candles, skulls with red paint on them, and giant red circles with strange markings surrounding it.

"What unholy sorcery is this?" Afomia was appalled.

"Okay, this is way too weird. I say we should get out as quickly..." Saanjh was saying as they heard a loud slamming sound.

"What was that?" Afomia asked.

"The door!" Saanjh realized as she looked at the Templar.

They both ran back to where the stairs were and found that the door had been shut.

"It's locked! What are we going to do?"

While the Mage was stressing out, Afomia could hear footsteps that did not sound human, approaching.

"Brace yourself, we have company." She warned.

Appearing before them was a creature that was only heard in myths, the Humbat. It was the size of a six foot human with wings on its arms. It stood on two legs and had sharp claws on its feet. Finally, its face was reminiscent of a bat.

"What foul beast is this?" Afomia asked.

"I don't know, but it's going down!" Saanjh jumped in front and casted her first spell. "FIREBALL!" However, instead of what she said, she shot out a rock that bounced off the creature, having no effect.

"What was that?" Afomia was confused.

"Uh, sorry. I forgot to tell you that I have this funny ability." The Mage said.

"And that is?"

"I never know what spell I will actually cast." The Mage said, giving her friend a worried look.

"You what?!"

The beast now pounced at the women but Afomia reacted by drawing her spear and smacking the enemy against the wall. She attempted to use her weapon to break the door but she felt some resistance as a magical barrier blocked her attack. Their problem would only continue as the monster shook off Afomia's attack.

Afomia stood ready to fight another round and Saanjh was about to join her. However, Afomia had other ideas.

"What are you doing? Let me at 'em!" Saanjh yelled.

"No, my spear won't work against whatever magical force that trapped us. I need you to find us a way out."

"Fine... but save some for me!"

As Saanjh left, the monster quickly charged at Afomia. The Templar held out her spear and the beast recklessly ran its chest into the weapon. Its eyes closed and all movement ceased, but it was only temporary.

Seconds later, the monster's eyes opened, which surprised Afomia. In her confusion, she didn't see her enemy retaliate, swinging its wing against her face. Afomia was slammed against the wall and she felt a cut across her right cheek. She wiped off the mark with her fingers and saw the creature running full speed at her. She got out of the way just in time as the monster rammed into the wall. Afomia dodged the heavy attack, but her opponent was far from finished as it shook off the sting.

Meanwhile, Saanjh surveyed the forcefield that had them trapped. She could sense that the caster who made it was of an elite calibre. She was struggling to find a solution as she heard a terrible screech from the monster.

"Afomia! Okay Saanjh, think, think, think!" She told herself with her eyes shut.

She was hoping to cast an energy blast at the barrier but instead, a small puff of cloud happened near her. She grew frustrated, but knowing Afomia was in danger, she resolved to one of her high risk spells.

The Humbat's call alerted two other creatures to its side. Afomia was able to swipe one aside but the other two simultaneously attacked her. One forced her to block with her spear and the other struck her left shoulder.

The templar was sent against her back on the ground. She attempted to get up and was limping on one knee. She held onto her spear staring down the three monstrosities that were about to strike her. Just as she was about to attack, she felt Saanjh grab her arm.

"What the? What are you doing back here?"

"There's no way for me to break the veil."

"Guess we have no choice but to..." Afomia couldn't finish as Saanjh interrupted.

"So hold on tight!"

"Wait what?!"

The three beasts pounced and their claws were an inch away from making contact. However, the two young women suddenly disappeared from sight and all three collided against the barrier.

Reappearing in the air were Afomia and Saanjh. They had teleported out the cabin and dropped on the ground.

"Oh my gosh. I can't believe that worked!" Saanjh was elated.

"You can teleport?!" Afomia was still in shock.

"Sort of..."

"Why didn't you do that sooner?!"

"Because I have no control over where I will end up. We could end up between a wall or maybe underwater..."

"Wow, we got very lucky then."

Saanjh held out her hand to Afomia. "Come on, we have to get you some medical attention."

"What are you talking about? I'm fine..." Suddenly, Afomia fainted.

"Afomia!" Saanjh caught her in time. As she did, Saanjh saw the injury on Afomia's shoulder. If she didn't find medical care for her ally soon, the wound could become fatal. Saanjh put Afomia on her back and made her way back to the village as dawn was rising.

Chapter 7: Brawl in the Library

U pon arriving at the library in the town, Ehsaas pulled on the door to find out it was locked. Unphased, he pulled out a metal pick from his pocket and used it on the door. He pulled out a lantern and lit it up before making his way through the shelves.

He quickly browsed through the books until he arrived at the back corner of the room. He pulled out the first hardcover book. Ehsaas blew off some dust and began flipping through the contents. The book contained ancient writings in a language he wasn't familiar with. However, he could decipher some of the weirdly drawn graphics. He could see claw marks and words that seem to resemble 'wolf' and 'man.'

Ehsaas pulled another book from the shelf and this one had a language that he understood. It was about a war between creatures known as Werewolves and Vampires. There was a war between two clans which took place in the town of Diamondvania. Not only was the town a battleground, it was also a place for them to grow their influence and expand their army.

Ehsaas was researching further until he heard a sound from the entrance of the library. He picked up his lantern and decided to investigate. He held the light source and saw a mysterious figure in a cloak.

"Library's closed. Can I help you?" Ehsaas called out.

"Oh really? Why are you here then, detective?" The man removed his hood.

"You're the chef from the kitchen. Shouldn't you be preparing dinner for your guests?"

"Oh don't worry detective. Dinner is ready, and it's about to be served." The chef was taking off his coak and his eyes were changing.

Ehsaas had his hand near his crossbow as he could hear footsteps from the sides. He knew the chef wasn't alone.

Suddenly, reaching out of the shelves was a claw that just missed Ehsaas's face. From behind, a werewolf attempted to sneak up on the hunter but Ehsaas launched a bolt and struck the enemy near the right clavicle. The beast felt a small sting and slowly, the pain intensified and it fainted.

"Silverbolt huh? You're pretty resourceful." Complimented the Chef.

"I got plenty more where that came from." the Archer threatened.

"Heh, you're going to need it."

Five more werewolves appeared in the small library. Ehsaas readied himself for battle, despite the fact he was at a huge disadvantage. He would much rather fight in open space but he didn't have much choice.

Ehsaas fired a bolt but this time it was swatted away. He launched a couple more but they were also deflected. He was slowly moving back until he felt his back against the wall. He had nowhere to run and the pack was closing in on him.

Seeing no way out, he threw the lantern above the werewolves. They were confused and Ehsaas took advantage by firing an arrow at the lantern. It created a small explosion, giving him a small window to escape past his enemies.

When the werewolf minions regained sight through the smoke, they were confused, but the Chef was not fooled. Using his sense of smell, he tracked where Ehsaas went and he hadn't gone far.

Ehsaas was running through the library with a book in his hand. Although it was quite dark, he could see where the exit was. However, as he approached the door, he was met with more werewolves there. He stopped and looked back to see the chef and other wolves there.

"End of the line, Detective." Chef Lycan said while the other werewolves were drooling.

Ehsaas pulled out his crossbow. "Do your worst."

Chef Lycan was about to command his wolves to attack, but he was interrupted by an eagle that had entered the room. The wolves were swinging their arms recklessly but they couldn't hit the eagle. Instead, most of them smacked each other and they quarreled amongst themselves.

Infuriated, Chef Lycan grabbed the eagle by the throat, and then slammed him to the ground. He was about to bite the feathered animal, but Ehsaas fired a silver bolt that forced the Chef to take a step back. That little delay allowed enough time for Olivia to appear and recall her companion back to her stone.

"Well well, what do we have here? Friend of yours?" He directed his question to Ehsaas who didn't answer him. "Tch whatever, my pack is hungry today. More food for them."

As they were making their advance, Ehsaas moved beside Olivia. "Hey, I don't know who you are, but thanks for saving me earlier."

"Don't mention it!" Olivia replied quickly.

"You should run though. I don't think I can beat these guys, but I should be able to stall for you."

"Stall? Oh no, we ain't running away after what he did to Max."

"Max? Oh that spirit eagle of yours."

"Yes! We need to avenge him!" Olivia exclaimed.

"Uh ok, but how are we going to..."

"Do you have any arrows?" The Summoner pressed the Archer.

"Yeah I got a few."

"Okay just give me some supporting fire."

"Alright..." Ehsaas was not confident.

In contrast, Olivia pulled out multiple summoning stones. She held them out and focused all her energy. The stones in her hands began to levitate and surge with power. Her eyes were beginning to glow and she called out an invocation.

"Lend me your strength, Sabir!"

Emerging out of the stones was a spirit elephant with massive tusks. It stomped on the ground multiple times before blowing its nose. Its sheer size and presence had the werewolves shaking at the knees.

Olivia hopped onto her giant companion's back, and together they charged towards their enemies. The wolves were so terrified, they were paralyzed.

The elephant took advantage of this opportunity and swung its tusk, knocking one of the werewolves hard against the ground.

Seeing their comrade defeated, the rest of the pack was ready to scatter, but Chef Lycan finally decided to take hold of the situation.

"Stop being cowards! Go back into formation and attack in unison!"

The werewolves did as they were told and as a unit, they charged at the elephant together. In addition, Chef Lycan let out a loud howl, which increased the morale of all the other werewolves. Suddenly, the giant elephant no longer seemed very frightening to the wolves.

Sabir was able to knock away two more werewolves but they were persistent, continuously climbing on its back. Little by little, they were causing pain to the elephant. Not only was the companion hurt, but Olivia felt everything as well. The leader of the wolves knew the drawbacks of the Summoner's powers, and he continued to order his minions to press the advantage.

The werewolves were just about to strike again, but a couple of them were shot down from the elephant by Ehsaas's silverbolts. That forced the attention back on him as the wolves changed their target.

One by one, they took turns trying to swipe at the Detective. He dodged all their attempts, but a few came close to hurting him, but instead, ripped his coat. He was in rhythm, but his body was getting exhausted and he had backed into a wall.

"Looks like this is the end of the road, Detective. Any last words?"

"As a matter of fact, I do."

"And what might they be?"

"Elephant stomp."

Chef Lycan had the look of confusion until he realized that he had completely forgotten about the elephant and his summoner. The Chef turned around to see Olivia calling out an attack.

"Seismic Storm!"

The elephant stomped the ground, and rock waves filled with dust began to hinder the wolves' vision. The wolves all covered their eyes and waited for the storm to pass. After a moment, the dust subsided but both the Detective and the Summoner had disappeared. Even the elephant had been recalled to his stones.

Chef Lycan knew they couldn't have gotten far. He ordered his lackeys to find their trail. However, as the wolves attempted to take their first big sniff, they all felt a burn through their airway. They whimpered in pain, which drove the leader mad.

"You imbeciles! What are you all..."

He took a whiff of the air and smelt something foul. He realized that the detective must have thrown something in the air before they escaped. As he was fuming, he could see that dawn was approaching within the hour. He directed his minions to retreat as he promised himself that he would hunt down the Summoner and the Detective during the next night.

Chapter 8: Unexpected Visitors

The next day had arrived, and within the town there was a middle aged doctor who treated the most severe medical injuries. He was in his office going through the report he had just written for his current patient.

"Your friend has sustained some serious wounds. What creature attacked the two of you?" the doctor asked.

"You won't believe me even if I told you." Replied Saanjh.

"Oh? I've been around and seen quite a bit. Try me."

"So there was this creature, it was half human half bat sort of..." Saanjh started off.

"A Humbat." The doctor stated confidently.

"Hum-what?"

"Humbat. Half human and half bat. A creature of the night that feeds on human blood." The doctor continued ignoring the shock on the girl's face.

"Whoa, how do you know all this?"

"Like I said, I've been around, and have seen injuries far worse than this."

"Oh, I'm sorry that I underestimated you." Saanjh apologized.

"Your friend has suffered several lacerations on her ribs. It's a good thing you got her to me when you did."

"Is she going to be okay?" Saanjh was worried.

"She seems like a tough fighter, so she should be fine. But I will need to keep her here for the night to ensure her recovery." The doctor suggested.

"Okay sounds good. Thank you Doctor...?"

"Acula. Doctor Acula."

Shortly after the exchange, Saanjh left the doctor's office. She figured now would be the best time to pick up some groceries as she was running low on supplies at home. She made her way to the marketplace nearby.

In the bazaar, there were many vendors selling various goods. There were many merchants, most were honest, but some would do anything to earn an extra silver coin or two.

Having lived here for sometime, Saanjh was not easily fooled. She remained focused on her grocery shopping, but what made it difficult were the strange stares she could receive and the whispers she would hear about herself.

"Look at that witch in her outfit." Someone whispered loudly.

"Better keep your distance or you might catch her bad fashion sense." They laughed together.

Saanjh walked away from the two villagers and then bumped into a child.

"I'm sorry. Are you okay?" She offered her hand to the little boy but her mom rushed in.

"Stay away from my boy!"

"Ma'am, I didn't mean to..." Saanjh attempted to apologize.

The woman didn't stay to speak with Saanjh, but the mage could hear the mother conversing with her son as they walked away. "My son, are you okay?! Where does it hurt?"

"I'm okay mama. Why are we walking away from the kind lady?" The boy questioned.

"Don't be deceived. That woman is a witch and will put a nasty curse on you." His mother warned.

Although Saanjh had heard similar words before, the pain still stung. Having done everything she needed to, she left the market and headed for home. The walk wasn't far, but it felt longer than most days.

When she arrived at her home, she opened the door and entered. Saanjh was hoping to relax after everything she had been through, but she felt something was off inside her house. She was about to look around but before she got the chance, someone tackled her to the ground.

Saanjh was about to yell but her mouth was being covered by someone's hand. She searched for the person and found the detective signalling for her to be quiet. The Mage was confused but obeyed for the moment.

With the Mage's compliance, Ehsaas poked his head so he could look through the window. When he saw that there was no one else outside, he let out a sigh of relief.

"Okay, the coast is clear." He told the mage.

Saanjh couldn't believe the audacity. "Excuse you, but who are you? And why are you in my house telling me to keep quiet?!"

"It's a long story, Miss Saanjh. Please calm down and let me explain." Ehsaas said calmly.

"I will not calm down! I demand to know... Hey, how did you know my name?" She narrowed her eyes on the young man.

"My name is Ehsaas, and I'm a detective called by the mayor to help solve the mysterious disappearances happening in Diamondvania."

"Huh, that sounds similar to Afomia." The Mage replied thinking of her friend.

"Pardon, who?" The Detective asked.

"Oh, Afomia, she's a templar knight sent here to investigate this town to complete her training." Saanjh replied.

Ehsaas continued, "Interesting, but anyway, I need to borrow your place because I have a friend who needs to rest her injuries."

"What?! You can't just barge in, take up my space and ask to borrow it after you have already done so! Besides, why does it have to be here?! Why me?"

"Out of everyone in this town, you're the safest bet." Ehsaas confirmed.

"Safest bet? What? You're making no sense."

"As part of my investigation, I had access to information about everyone in the town. Out of all the profiles I read, you were the least likely to be one of them."

"One of them? Of who?" Saanjh was even more confused.

At that moment, a howl could be heard outside of Saanjh's house.

"Them." Ehsaas said.

The Mage was trying to piece together what Ehsaas was saying. "You mean the wolves?"

"Not wolves, but werewolves."

"Wait what?! Where are they?!"

"Here in the town. They are disguised as regular people during the day, but when night falls, that's when their true colours are revealed." The detective filled her in.

"I knew there was something fishy going on. But why are they here?" The Mage asked.

Ehsaas threw a book over to Saanjh and she flipped to the page she was told. What she saw were werewolves battling against vampires in ancient art.

"The werewolves and vampires are at war with each other and Diamondvania is their battleground." Ehsaas explained.

"But this book is so old. There is no way this war could be going on for so long..." Saanjh had an epiphany in the middle of her sentence. "The ritual circle in the cabin..."

"Hopefully, you understand now. Don't trust anyone who lives here too easily."

Again Saanjh had a thought, but this time she also felt a massive pit in her stomach. "Oh no, I left Afomia with the doctor!"

"What was the doctor's name?"

"Doctor Acula."

Ehsaas grabbed the book and flipped through the pages. He was hoping not to find a specific name in the book. Unfortunately, his worst fear was realized when he found the page with the information he did not want to see.

"Your friend is in trouble." He said as the colour in his face drained.

"We have to save her!" Saanjh panicked.

"We can't. My friend is still resting, and we can't leave her alone."

"Umm, Is that your friend there?" The Mage pointed.

They both saw Olivia standing in the room with bandages covering her body.

"Olivia, what are you doing? You still need rest." The Detective said firmly.

Olivia took a breath. "I heard everything. Let's go and save her friend."

"You would do that for someone you just met?" Saanjh was in disbelief.

"Yeah, why not? You seem like a good person." Olivia replied without hesitation. The Mage was speechless.

"Sigh, alright, but we have to get this done before dusk. Once it's nightfall..." Ehsaas started to say.

"Yeah yeah, big mean wolves will attack us. Let's go!" The Summoner finished.

Olivia led the charge, followed by Saanjh, and finally Ehsaas.

Chapter 9: New Patients

Inside the doctor's office, there was a door where no visitors were allowed to pass without his permission. As the doctor entered the room, he closed the door behind him.

This room had no windows and was completely shut out from sunlight. It was a decent sized room filled with stone coffins. Inside each one was an unconscious human lying inside. One of which was Afomia.

The doctor walked through the entire room, taking a good look at all his patients. As he moved, some of the bats that were hanging in the ceiling flew down and hovered around him. He stopped at one of his patients, who was a female, the same one that was attacked by her boyfriend turned werewolf. There was a bite mark on her neck that resembled that of a vampire's teeth.

The doctor took off his mask and gloves, revealing a middle aged pale face man. He began lifting his hands up.

"Arise, my child."

Upon his call, the woman's eyes opened wide. Her skin was extremely pale, but when she stood up from the coffin, she looked very much awake and alive.

The doctor was smiling, seeing that he had added a new recruit to his following. However, his enjoyment would be cut short as one of his bats landed on his shoulder. It whispered into his ear.

"It appears we have visitors. Time to welcome our guests." The doctor said aloud.

STANDING OUTSIDE WERE the Summoner, Magician, and the Detective. The sun was beginning to set and in front of them was the doctor's office. It had a sign on the door that read, 'Closed'.

"This is the place." Saanjh confirmed.

"Looks like he took the day off." Olivia replied.

"No worries, it won't take me long." Ehsaas said as he pulled out a metal pick. However, before he could get his hands on the door, it opened. Everyone was on guard until Saanjh and Olivia saw the person who greeted them.

"It's you! From back in the forest!" Olivia exclaimed.

"Wait, how do you know her?" Saanjh questioned.

"I brought her back from the forest the other day along with her boyfriend." The Summoner explained.

"That was you?!" The Mage said, amazed.

Their conversation was interrupted by the woman welcoming them. "My master has been expecting you."

She turned around expecting them to follow. However, Ehsaas, Olivia, and Saanjh all looked at the woman incredulously, and then at each other.

"This is obviously a trap." Ehsaas stated.

"But my friend is in there!" Saanjh urged.

"I know, but..." Ehsaas was hesitant, but Olivia jumped in.

"Let's follow her."

"This is an awful idea." Ehsaas tried to reason with them.

"Don't worry. Between the three of us, I'm sure we can take on some old doctor." Olivia sounded confident.

The woman stopped in the hall when she realized the three visitors were still at the entrance.

"Please follow me. My master wishes to speak with you." The pale servant reiterated.

Saanjh and Olivia were the first to enter. When Ehsaas saw his two allies setting foot inside, he reluctantly went with them.

The guide had a lit candle and guided them through the halls. Nothing seemed out of the ordinary until they arrived at a door at the end. It was a typical door but all three visitors could sense a disturbing presence beyond it.

Once they entered, they could see no windows in the room. The only light source were candles spread throughout. Also, there were multiple coffins, all of them were closed, except for one that was empty.

"Afomia is in one of these coffins. I can sense it." Saanjh whispered to them.

"Okay, let's quickly find the one and..." Ehsaas was interrupted as the doctor appeared out of the shadows from the corner of the room.

"Welcome! My apologies for the crowded room. It gives a nice cozy atmosphere, which I very much enjoy."

"Where is Afomia?!" Saanjh was ready to fight but Olivia held her back.

"Don't worry about your friend. Like I promised, I've kept her to ensure she makes a quick recovery."

"You better not have done anything to harm her or I'll hurt you so bad, you won't want to be a doctor anymore!" Saanjh continued with her anger but Ehsaas interrupted, hoping to calm her down.

"You can drop the act. I know you aren't a real doctor." Ehsaas pressed.

"How could you make such an accusation? I know much about human blood and have studied human anatomy longer than any human being has. I'm more than qualified to be called a doctor."

"You are right. You probably have more knowledge about the human body than any other person. Helps when you are immortal, doesn't it?"

"Oh! So you really do know who I am." The doctor was impressed.

"Yes, you can stop with the games. Lord of Vampires."

The doctor smiled and clapped his hands. He congratulated the Detective for figuring out his identity.

"So, as a prize for guessing who you are correctly, we get Saanjh's friend back and a free pass out of here?" Olivia was hoping.

"Tch, I'm afraid not." The doctor smirked.

"Well, it was worth a shot." Olivia shrugged.

"Actually, I want to extend an invitation to all of you."

"For what, a party?" Olivia questioned.

"No, he wants us to join his army." Ehsaas answered.

"Why would he need us?" Olivia was confused.

"Because he has a feud against the werewolves. In order for him to win this war, he needs more followers." Ehsaas added.

"That is correct! My my, you just have everything figured out, don't you Detective? Now what do you say? Will you join my army?" The doctor asked excitedly.

As he gave the offer, he pointed their attention to the woman who guided them here. Her skin looked pale and something about her felt unnatural, like she was no longer human.

"I'm guessing we are going to end up like her if we accept." Olivia asked, and Ehsaas nodded. "And if we reject, he will most likely eliminate us huh? Ehsaas agreed again.

While they were mulling over their choice, Saanjh jumped in. "You can take your invitation and shove it up your..."

"Saanjh!" They both yelled at her.

"What? I was going to say coffin." She rolled her eyes.

Suddenly, the door behind them slammed shut and locked. The doctor snapped his fingers, and out of half the coffins in the room, awoke the villagers that had been bitten on their necks. They crawled out with their mouths opened, showing two sharp fangs. They had been turned into vampires.

Saanjh, Ehsaas, and Olivia stood together as their enemies were slowly trying to surround them. While Ehsaas and Olivia were preparing to fight, Saanjh couldn't help but notice that someone was missing in the crowd."

"Where's Afomia?" Saanjh demanded.

"Oh your friend? She is right here!" The doctor said proudly.

The Count lifted his right hand and Afomia levitated unconsciously out of a remaining coffin. Using his telekinetic power, the Vampire Lord moved the Templar in front of him. He opened his mouth and was about to bite her neck.

"No!" Saanjh was held back by both her allies.

"I'm sorry Saanjh, but we can't save her..." Olivia solemnly apologized.

His fangs were about to make contact against her neck but before it could, a mystical light barrier appeared around Afomia. The vampire attempted to bite the templar but as his fangs made contact on the barrier of light, he felt a burning pain in his mouth.

"What happened?" Olivia was curious about the turn of events.

"Afomia is a templar! She must have an ability that protects her!" Saanjh spoke excitedly.

The Vampire Lord was still shaken and his minions were waiting for his command. In their idleness, Ehsaas pulled out a bottle of clear liquid and threw it in the air. He then fired an arrow at the glass and shattered it, sprinkling all the liquid on the minions. As it made contact on their pale skin, the creatures screamed in pain.

"What is that stuff?" The Summoner wondered.

"Holy Water."

"Wow, you are prepared for everything." Olivia was impressed.

"I only have a bit left. Let's use this opportunity to grab her friend and get out. I have a feeling the Templar's ability won't activate again."

Saanjh looked around and saw Afomia's weapon in the corner. "I'll grab her spear!"

Olivia and Ehsaas ran to the coffin where the templar was resting. The Summoner put Afomia on her back and carried her out, with Ehsaas holding his bow, ready for supporting fire. Saanjh followed behind.

A locked door blocked their way, so Olivia pulled out two of her summoning stones to call for help. The stones lit up, clashed together and out of the combined energy, she called forth a rhino.

"Nicholas, charge through that door!" She commanded.

The horned companion obeyed and slammed through with ease. Olivia, Ehsaas, and Saanjh ran through together. Now that they had escaped the office, they thought they were safe. Unfortunately, meeting them outside were a horde of werewolves, led by their commander.

Seeing their numbers, the three fighters were about to turn back, but rushing out of the office were the minions of vampires with their master standing behind. They were surrounded and were preparing for the worst. However, a thick tension filled the air.

Chef Lycan and the Count locked eyes, which woke a storm that had been brewing for centuries. The werewolves and vampires charged and clashed against one another. Caught in the crossfire were Saanjh, Ehsaas, and Olivia. They were trying to find a way out, but things got complicated when Nicholas, Olivia's rhino, took collateral damage from the armies fighting and was sent back to the summoning stones.

As a result of the companion's defeat, Olivia felt a surge of pain through her body. Now, both the Summoner and Templar knight had their movement severely hindered. Ehsaas was low on ammunition and he was also out of ideas.

That left Saanjh looking for a solution. She considered using her teleportation ability but her energy was low, and she had reservations about her spells working on four people. However, with the army of werewolves and vampires in a frenzy, the mage was ready to use her last resort.

However, her focus was interrupted as a Humbat pounced towards them. The Mage was unable to cast her spell, the detective was in no position to help her, the Summoner was too injured and the Templar remained unconscious. They were helpless to the creature that was about to tear them to shreds.

Chapter 10: Diamondvania

Afomia slowly opened her eyes. She wasn't sure how long she had been out for, but she could feel her strength had weakened due to lack of use. Holding her head with one hand, she looked around and realized she was in a cavern.

She was trying to get up until she saw a grotesque zombie creature reaching its hand towards her. Her training allowed her to react by evading then grabbing its hand. She then kicked the beast in the pelvic region and dashed away as the monster grimaced in pain.

She ran through the caverns with haste, but she could not find the way out. Instead, she was met with other monstrous creatures: a mummy, a scarecrow, and a creature covered by a potato sack.

Without her spear, she had to resort to her alternative method of combat. She clapped her hands together and a ray of light imbued her fist with holy energy. With this new power, she began throwing punches at her enemies.

Afomia overpowered her enemies with ease, to the point she felt they weren't even trying to fight back. She had all three monsters on the ropes and was about to finish them, when suddenly, a mysterious man wearing a cloak stood between her and the creatures.

"That's enough. Leave these poor beings alone." The man's voice had authority.

Afomia was baffled, she was wondering why a human would be protecting the hideous monsters.

"I don't know who you are, but step aside. Those vile beings must be cleansed." The man would not budge to Afomia's demand. "You leave me no choice then." She pushed forward.

Channeling her energy into her fist, she attempted to punch the mysterious man in the face. She was inches away from landing the hit, but as she got closer, she felt time was slowing down. It was a feeling she never had before and it felt like an eternity before her fist would make contact against her enemy.

In contrast, she saw her enemy move at normal speed to react to her attack. He was going to evade her attack successfully and follow up with a punch of his own. As the counterattack approached Afomia, she could see a flashback of her entire life in the monastery. All her childhood growing up with her brothers, and training with her teachers and Master Ruthar were replaying in her mind.

She was lost in a deep trance until she heard a faint voice that slowly grew louder with time. "Afomia. Afomia. AFOMIA!"

Finally, the templar snapped out of the flashback and was conscious in the present time. She looked around and saw that Saanjh was the one calling her name. Standing in front of her though, was the mysterious man who had his fist right in front of her face. She realized the man had withheld his attack and if he didn't, she wouldn't be conscious right now.

"Heh, not bad. You didn't cower in fear." The man said.

He pulled back his hand and began walking away. As he did, Saanjh jumped and gave Afomia a big hug. "Afomia!"

"Hey, I missed you too." Afomia said as she looked up and saw a couple others she didn't recognize. "Who are they?"

"They're friends of ours. In fact, they helped save your life." Saanjh said.

"Save me? From what?"

"Looks like we have a lot to catch her up on." Ehsaas spoke.

"Anyone want to volunteer to recap for her?" asked Saanjh.

"I'll do it!" Olivia gladly stepped up and began to tell Afomia everything that happened while she was unconscious.

OLIVIA AND EHSAAS COULD only watch as a Humbat pounced into the air, about to slash Saanjh, who was completely defenseless. The mage closed her eyes, expecting the worst, but crashing into the battlefield was a horse pulling a buggy with its mysterious cloaked rider holding the reins. As they made their entrance, they knocked aside a few vampires and werewolves before slamming the Humbat out of the way. The rider then looked to the three conscious fighters and told them, "Get on."

Ehsaas and Saanjh were skeptical, but out of desperation, they knew staying to fight was not an option. Saanjh helped Olivia up onto the wagon while Ehsaas went to get Afomia. As he was carrying the templar, the vengeful Humbat got back up and attempted to attack them again.

Saanjh was in no position to help, but the cloaked rider was. He intercepted the Humbat and stopped the creature with one hand. He then struck the beast with a roundhouse kick, and threw the monster against some of the other enemies.

Both Ehsaas and Saanjh were shocked by what had just happened. In contrast, the rider dusted his hands without breaking a sweat. He then took the reins and commanded the horse to leave. Together, they all escaped the battlefield and went into the forest.

AFTER OLIVIA WAS FINISHED with the summary, Afomia turned to the mysterious man. "I'm sorry for my rash actions earlier. Thank you for saving me."

"Don't mention it. Get some rest, you still aren't fully healed yet." As he was leaving, Olivia spoke up.

"Hold on, you said you would tell us what's going on after our friend woke up."

"Heh, you have a pretty good memory." The man had forgotten. "Alright, a deal is a deal. You better sit down, this might be a lot to take in."

CENTURIES AGO, DIAMONDVANIA was a place ravaged by monstrous creatures throughout the land. Vampires, werewolves, zombies, witches, and all sorts of creatures fought for survival. Humans who lived during this era were great warriors that fought every moment of their lives to survive another day. This made them incredibly resilient and strong.

As time passed, the monsters divided into factions with the vampires and werewolves having the strongest armies. Their strength overpowered all the other monsters and scattered them throughout the land. This caused the two factions to be at war with one another, creating absolute chaos through the land.

Meanwhile, as human forces were dwindling, they had discovered a way to stop the two factions. On the day that the vampires and werewolves gathered their entire armies to end their dispute, the human mages combined their magic and casted a spell that created a portal and trapped all the vampires and werewolves inside. The spell was successful, so successful in fact, that it also trapped all the other monsters throughout the land as well.

With no monsters roaming the lands of Diamondvania, the humans had achieved a peaceful utopia. Or so they thought.

As time passed, the people of Diamondvania began to value trading, status, and above all, comfort. People who knew magic and practiced it became ostracised. Overtime, they grew weak as the number of fighters dwindled everyday.

However, there was one mage, a necromancer to be exact, who hated living in this time. He grew disdain for the people of Diamondvania, who bullied him every chance they got. Seeking revenge, he practiced his dark magic in secrecy, out in the forest inside a cabin.

His powers grew stronger but more importantly, he found out about the portal used to seal away the monsters. He made it his life's work to resummon the horrors from centuries ago.

"I GUESS WE CAN SAY, he succeeded." Saanjh threw in.

"Not entirely." The cloaked man said.

"What do you mean?" Afomia was confused.

"He only succeeded in opening the portal for a short amount of time. A vast majority of the vampires and werewolves armies are still locked away."

"You mean there are more of them?!" Olivia was shocked.

"That would be problematic. We already had so much difficulty with the few that were here." Ehsaas assessed.

"It's okay, we don't have to worry about that portal opening." Saanjh said confidently.

"And why is that?" The Summoner wondered.

"I heard tales about that necromancer. He got chased out of the town and fell off a cliff. He's dead."

"Presumed to be dead." The mysterious man added.

"You mean to say he is still alive?" Ehsaas asked.

"Just a possibility to consider."

What the man said left everyone wondering, but as they were deep in thought, he stood up and was ready to leave. However, Afomia interrupted him one last time.

"Hey, what is your name?"

"Ah, it's been awhile since anyone has asked me that. Call me Rice." He replied and turned to leave. "Oh, and get some rest." Rice added.

After he had left the room the four friends were alone around a bonfire.

"What do you all think?" Ehsaas asked everyone.

"There is something he isn't telling us." Saanjh suspected.

"What?! Are you two saying he's our enemy?" Olivia blurted out loud then covered her mouth, realizing she was a bit loud.

"Hey, it's like he said, it's a possibility to consider." Ehsaas was imitating what Rice had said earlier.

"I don't think he's our enemy." They all looked at Afomia who spoke with confidence.

"What makes you say that?" Saanjh wanted to know.

"He's way stronger than us and could have easily struck us down when we were vulnerable. In addition, he saved us and gave us a place to rest. At the very least, we have to thank him for that."

Afomia had a very valid point, and no one could argue what she had to say. It was also getting late and fatigue was beginning to sink in. Starting with Ehsaas, he stood to leave, and told everyone to rest up for the next day. Olivia went next, leaving Saanjh and Afomia.

Saanjh got up for a moment to grab something before quickly returning back to Afomia. "Here, we kept this safe for you."

Afomia received her spear back from Saanjh. "Thank you."

Saanjh left after that, leaving Afomia to herself. She began to reflect about her actions towards the monsters she fought earlier in the day.

"Maybe they aren't the real monsters..."

Chapter 11: Training

After a good night's rest, Afomia woke up from the cave feeling rejuvenated. She thought she would be the first one up but to her surprise, she didn't see Saanjh, Olivia, or Ehsaas resting nearby. Not wanting to lose her reputation of being a disciplined warrior, she grabbed her weapon and made her way through the cavern.

Just like before, she was struggling to find the way out. The place felt like a labyrinth and she was growing frustrated. Out of her anger, she kicked what she thought was a puddle. However, something flew out of the puddle and it smacked against the wall. It then slowly slid down the wall and fell to the ground.

Realizing that she possibly severely injured an innocent creature, she rushed to check on its status. When she arrived at the spot, she saw a unique monster, a green jelly blob with its eyes closed.

"I'm sorry, it was an accident! Are you alright?"

The green jelly slime opened its eyes, which were black with no pupils. It saw Afomia and smiled at her, accepting her apology. Then it quickly bounced back up, indicating that Afomia caused it no harm.

"Phew, thank goodness." Afomia returned the smile.

It stuck out one of its arms, holding it out for a handshake. Afomia saw its hand and was a bit grossed out. However, after kicking it earlier, she felt obligated to shake its hand. She reached out reluctantly and shook the creature's limb while closing her eyes and facing away.

After the handshake was complete, the slime slid in a circle, doing a dance, celebrating the fact it had made a new friend. At the same time, Afomia had an epiphany.

"Hey blobby, do you think you can show me where my friends went?"

The slime had to process what Afomia had said. Once it had been given a moment, it nodded its head excitedly.

"Can you lead me to them?"

Filled with enthusiasm, the blob began sliding quickly and leading the way. Afomia nearly lost sight of the green jelly but thankfully, it left a green liquid trail behind for her to follow.

OUTSIDE THE CAVE, CLOUDS filled the afternoon sky. Olivia had found a river and released her companions out to play. She could see many of the animals enjoying themselves, until a small altercation occurred.

It started with the wolf and rhinoceros exchanging growls and roars against another. Then slowly, all the other animals joined in and began voicing their discontent. Olivia had to intervene.

"Everyone stop! What's gotten into all of you?"

Her voice was not reaching them, so she had to resort to pulling out her stones and recalling them all back. When she had successfully got them all back safely, she looked at her summoning stones. She couldn't figure out what caused them to lash out, but she had a feeling something ominous must have been nearby.

THE GREEN SLIME HAD led Afomia outside the cavern, where she heard a noise. The templar told the slime to keep quiet as she subtly made her way to the source of the sound. Hiding up in a tree, she saw two people fighting, one of them was Ehsaas, who was sent hard against the ground.

"Alright, we are done for today." Rice decided.

"No. I can still keep going." Ehsaas did not want the training to end.

"You've attempted fifty times already with similar results each time. Your fifty-first try won't end any differently. Go rest for the day."

Rice turned his back and began walking. Ehsaas wasn't satisfied, he held up his crossbow and aimed it at his target. The Detective fired the arrow with Afomia watching in the trees. She was worried about Rice who seemed vulnerable.

As the arrow got within range, Rice turned around and grabbed the arrow with his right hand. He then appeared in front of Ehsaas. The Detective was unable to move as his opponent held the arrow and pointed it to his neck.

Afomia, who saw all this, was about to shout to call off the fight, but the blob creature held her back. It assured her that everything would be alright.

"You're persistent, I'll give you that." Rice retracted the arrow.

"It's not enough! You and I both know that!" Ehsaas stomped the ground in frustration.

"Tell me, why are you so hell-bent on wanting to grow stronger?" Rice questioned.

"Unlike the others, I have no special powers to rely on. Olivia has her summons, Afomia has her holy magic, and Saanjh can cast spells. I'm just an ordinary person. That is why I need to keep training, so I don't become a liability." The young Archer admitted.

"Admirable. Very well, we can resume your training." The man replied, impressed.

"Thank you." Ehsaas was ready to fight again, but Rice told him to wait a moment.

"Your opponent won't be me."

Confused, Ehsaas asked, "Huh? But there is no one else here."

Rice threw the arrow towards the tree. He missed Afomia on purpose, but the arrow barely missed her face. The sudden surprise caused her to lose balance and she fell off the tree and onto a bush.

"She will be your opponent." Rice pointed at the templar.

"Afomia?! Wait, how long were you hiding up there for?" Ehsaas called out.

"Oww... not long." She replied.

"Well, you better get up quick. I'm not a very patient person." Ehsaas stated.

"Wait, you don't seriously think you can take me on." Afomia said in disbelief.

Ehsaas pulled one of his bolts and loaded it onto his crossbow.

"Ha, fine. But don't say I didn't warn you!"

Afomia readied her spear, preparing to battle her ally. She struck first, rushing straight at the Detective. She thought it was going to be an easy victory, but Ehsaas threw down multiple glass bottles that shattered against the ground.

Suddenly, the once clear battlefield was covered in smoke. Afomia held her spear with two hands, and began to whirl it around. It created a huge gust which cleared the field but Ehsaas was no longer in Afomia's sight. As she was looking around, an arrow was approaching her but the templar deflected it away with her spear.

"Hiding in the trees? What a cowardly move." scoffed the templar.

"Fighting you head on would be a fool's strategy. You and I both know that." The bowman responded.

"Guess you have a point. Also, thank you." Afomia said with a grin.

"For what?" The young man didn't have time to switch into defense.

Afomia slammed her weapon against a tree and Ehsaas dropped onto the ground near her. When he looked up, he was met with the spear near his face.

"For telling me where you were. If you had kept your mouth shut, I wouldn't have found you."

"Heh, and here I thought you were all muscle and no brains." Ehsaas teased.

"Oh, there is more to me than meets the eye. Now, do you have any last words?"

"Yeah, you should really watch your step." Ehsaas was now the person with the smile.

Afomia looked down and saw a loose rope around her feet. Before she knew it, she was tied up by rope and lifted off the ground, hanging upside down from the tree.

"What the? How?" She struggled.

The boy laughed, "I can't believe you walked into that one."

"Using traps too?" Afomia rolled her eyes.

"Hey, I got no powers, remember? Got to use every resource to even the playing field."

"Hm, fair point. I'll admit, you are resourceful."

"So you surrender?" Ehsaas asked.

"I hate to disappoint you, but no."

"What? But you have no way of getting out!"

"Like I said before, you should really keep your mouth shut." Afomia untied the rope, dropping down but landed on her feet.

"How did you...?" The Archer couldn't believe it.

"Next time, I suggest you tie a triple knot." Afomia replied with confidence.

Ehsaas held up his crossbow while Afomia reclaimed her spear. They were at a standoff, waiting for the other to make their next move. However, their focus would be broken as they felt the ground shake beneath their feet.

Out of the ground, multiple skeletal hands burst from the cracks. A couple reached out and grabbed both Afomia and Ehsaas by their legs.

Afomia was able to use her spear to break loose. In contrast, Ehsaas was being pulled down by the arm.

He would have been dragged down below but the green slime bounced onto the skeletal arm. As a result, Ehsaas's leg slipped away and he was free.

"Way to go, Slimy!" Afomia high-fived the blob.

Their small celebration wouldn't last as the army of skeletons emerged from below the surface.

"What are these?" Ehsaas asked in distress.

"Skeleton minions. He must be close." Rice answered the detective.

Afomia had her spear ready to fight the undead horde as was Ehsaas holding his crossbow but Rice stepped in.

"I'll handle this. Your powers aren't sufficient yet to deal against them. He directed that comment to Afomia and then he turned to Ehsaas. "And I have a feeling you don't have anything in your bag of tricks to deal against these foes."

Ehsaas didn't want to admit it, but Rice was correct. "What do you want us to do then?"

"Go back to the cavern, make sure all the creatures are safe."

Afomia and the slime acknowledged what they had to do and left with haste. Ehsaas was about to follow but Rice had one more thing to add.

"Wait." Ehsaas stopped at the sternness of Rice's voice. "Don't let them take Saanjh."

Ehsaas didn't know the gravity of the situation, but he knew Rice was serious. He nodded and left the clearing.

Chapter 12: Loss

After setting her companions down and returning them to their stones, Olivia was nearing the caverns. Upon her return, she was met with an unexpected sight. She saw a stranger wearing torn mage robes with red markings all over his skin.

Olivia approached with caution until she noticed that the man had someone captured. The captive had her mouth sealed, limbs binded by a dark binding spell, and she was unconscious.

"Saanjh! You let her go right now!" The Summoner demanded.

Seeing the man refuse, Olivia called out her wolf and eagle companion.

"Saanvi, attack him from the front. Max, take to the sky and give him an aerial assault! Show him no mercy!"

She imbued the wolf with extra ferocity and the eagle with extra speed. The duo were about to strike, but the man lifted one hand and the marks on his body began to glow. A dark red flash caused Olivia to quickly cover her eyes. When she opened them, she saw both her companions lying on the ground, unable to move.

The Dark Mage aimed to obliterate the two creatures, while Olivia pulled out her stones to try and reclaim them into their stones. She managed to save Saanvi, but Max suffered a terrible fate. Olivia could only watch as one of her loyal friends slowly faded to dust. In her despair, she lost all restraint and Sabir appeared out of his stone without Olivia's command; he came to avenge Max.

The elephant ran full speed at the enemy but the mage was ready to counter-attack. A summoning circle appeared from the ground and emerging from it was a skeletal mammoth. It clashed against Sabir and they were stuck in a deadlock.

They seemed evenly matched for a moment, until the dark summoner empowered his mammoth with an unholy frenzy spell. The mammoth's strength doubled and it went berserk. Sabir was no match and was tossed aside. He tried to get up but the mammoth relentlessly stomped on his body.

Seeing such a sight, Olivia attempted to recall him back, but the infernal mage had another trick. He casted a curse on Sabir that prevented him from returning to his summoning stone. The mammoth continued to stomp on Sabir; Olivia fell to the ground. She felt every ounce of pain that her animal companion experienced.

The malicious mage had won and saw no reason to stay. He took his captive, Saanjh, and left, leaving his mammoth to finish his foes. Despite lying on the ground in excruciating pain, Olivia reached out her hand, trying to stop the enemy from escaping.

"Saanjh..." she said with a strangled breath. She watched as the malevolent mage took her captured friend and disappeared into the distance.

The skeletal mammoth could see its counterpart no longer responsive and was about to land the crushing blow. Another one of Olivia's companions was about to be vanquished, but an arrow diverted the mammoth's attention.

Ehsaas had arrived but the mammoth was not intimidated by his presence. It charged full speed at the Detective, thinking he had no way to stop its rampage. However, appearing to block its path was Afomia, who dropped one end of her spear to the ground. There was a sudden flash of radiant light that blinded the mammoth and caused it to trip on its own feet.

It was only a momentary win as the mammoth regained its footing and wildly sung its tusks, striking both his enemies. Both Ehsaas and Afomia were struggling to move and their gigantic foe towered over them. It had its sight set on their destruction but out of nowhere, Sabir was granted one last burst of energy when Olivia transferred her remaining energy to the elephant. Sabir sent full force against the mammoth and his tusks struck the beast. It was the final hit that caused the skeletal creature to dissipate.

Both Ehsaas and Afomia let out a sigh of relief. Then they made their way to their ally.

"Olivia! Are you okay? Talk to us!" Afomia was worried but thankfully, the Summoner was able to reply weakly.

"I'm sorry. I couldn't stop him..."

"Him? Wait, where is Saanjh?"

"He took her..."

"Who took her?" Ehsaas wanted to know but Olivia had fainted.

Now, appearing before them was Rice. He lifted Olivia and started towards the cavern, but before he could enter Ehsaas had something to say.

"You know who did this, don't you?" The man stopped for a moment.

Afomia stared at both Ehsaas and Rice, waiting for someone to break the silence.

"Let's get your friend stabilized first." Rice said gravely.

He continued walking into the cavern with Olivia over his shoulder. Afomia followed after to see if she could help. The last to enter was Ehsaas, who waited patiently for more answers.

Chapter 13: Abducted

M*oments earlier...*
        In another part of the forest, Saanjh was practising her magic alone. Her spell would begin with potential, but the end result would always be a flop. It would either fizzle out or randomly cast a different spell that she didn't want. The frustration for her was piling on.

"Ugh! Why?! Why can't I get it right?!" She fell on one knee and punched the ground.

When she looked up to get back to her training, she saw a man wearing mage robes with strange red markings through his body.

"Uh, can I help you?" Saanjh asked the strange man.

"No. Actually, the reason I'm here is to help you."

"Right... Sorry mister, but I know better than to talk to strang..."

Before she could finish, the man casted a spell and a magical energy orb hovered above the palm of his hand. Saanjh was mesmerized by how he could control his power with ease. She wanted to learn how.

"You... you're a magician!" She exclaimed.

"One of the few, sadly." The man responded.

"What happened to everyone?"

"After all the monsters disappeared, there was no longer any need for our kind. Some went into hiding, but many of us are not part of this world anymore."

"That's so sad..." the young mage said.

"Don't worry, their sacrifices will not be for nothing." The man said eerily.

"What do you mean? What are you planning?" Saanjh had a terrible feeling.

"Those ungrateful swines are about to experience what life was like centuries ago. A place filled with terrifying creatures that feed on the weak!" The man yelled.

Saanjh jerked away, startled, she then had a flashback to when she was in the hidden basement. "The ritual..."

"Ah, so you know. Excellent." The older mage wore a sinister smile.

"But how will releasing those horrors help our kind?" Saanjh asked feeling unsure.

"Once the creatures ravage the peasants' homes, our brethren will rise and rid the world of these abominations. Everyone will know and remember the power of the magicians!" The vile mage said proudly.

"No, this isn't right. You can't do this!" Saanjh urged.

"So you rather side with those fools who made our people's lives miserable?"

"I'm not saying they were right, but there has to be a better way!"

"Tch, I once thought similar to you, but those villagers are far too arrogant. They must be severely punished."

"Then I can't allow your plans to happen." Saanjh took her fighting stance.

"Please, we both know the end results if we were to fight." The man scoffed.

"Sounds like someone is scared."

The man was somewhat impressed by the young woman's stubbornness and thought it would be a shame to not have her as an ally.

"I'll give you one last chance. Join me." He held out his hand hoping she would accept.

"Let me think..."

Saanjh pretended, and then suddenly launched a fire blast spell. Her spell changed and turned into a frost bolt that struck the man's left arm, freezing part of his elbow.

"Your spell level is amateur at best." He made a fist with his left hand and broke off the ice.

Saanjh was not deterred, she was about to cast another spell but her enemy reacted by casting a curse to seal Saanjh's mouth. Then, dark ribbons appeared and wrapped around the female magician. Despite being in such a bind, Saanjh continued to struggle to break free.

"You have a strong will, but that alone will never be enough to defeat me." The evil magician mocked.

He lifted his hand and out from the ground appeared a skeletal brute. Its order was to carry Saanjh and it obeyed. It was walking away, holding the struggling young mage in its arms when Olivia appeared.

From there, the malicious magician easily dealt with her summons and called out his skeletal mammoth to finish her off. Seeing that his undead minion had the situation under control, he left the clearing with his prize.

While heading to his hideout with his captive in tow he felt a sudden change to his energy level. He realized that his mammoth had been defeated.

"Perhaps I underestimated them." He thought to himself briefly before he continued on his way.

Chapter 14: Prisoners

It was a beautiful sunny day in the open fields. All the animals had been let out of their stones to play. They were all very energetic and chasing each other in the grass. Everyone was having a great time and Olivia was smiling as she watched on.

After calling all the animals over, they piled on top of her for a massive hug. She was extremely happy as she looked at each one of their eyes, until she saw Max.

Suddenly, she began seeing flashes of the eagle lying on the ground with critical injuries. The images were haunting her mind and Olivia began to go insane. She held her head and swung her body around. As she continued, she flung herself into the river, where she descended into the deep dark abyss. She was drowning and eventually, she lost her breath.

Olivia's eyes flew open and she found herself in a cold sweat. It took her a moment to realise that she had woken from a nightmare. Nevertheless, the grief of losing her eagle companion Max settled in.

"Olivia! You're awake!" Afomia arrived first.

"We were worried about you there." Ehsaas stood nearby with his arms crossed.

"What happened?" Olivia asked, trying to collect herself.

"You saved us from the giant mammoth. You have my thanks for that." Afomia lowered her head.

Olivia covered her eyes and began to cry.

"What's wrong?" Ehsaas wasn't sure why she burst into tears.

"My eagle. I lost him..." She held out his summoning stone, which no longer had the symbols engraved.

Afomia wrapped her arm around Olivia to give her some comfort. Ehsaas immediately turned his sight to Rice, who stood there and hadn't said a word.

"You! This is your fault!" Ehsaas shouted suddenly.

"Ehsaas, what are you talking about?" Afomia was shocked by his accusation.

"He knows the person who took Saanjh!"

Olivia stopped to look up with tears still in her eyes. Both she and Afomia gave questioning looks at Rice, who kept silent. They gave him a moment before he felt the need to respond.

"It's true, I once knew him."

"Who is he?" Olivia grew curious.

"His name is Bal. He was once a highly respected magician who helped Diamondvania combat against the monsters that roamed the lands." Rice continued.

"What happened during that time?" Afomia asked.

Rice prepared himself to tell a story about the past. "Along with a few other mages, we sealed the monsters away, inside the portal. However, many sacrifices were made that day."

"That happened centuries ago. How could both of you still be alive?" Olivia wasn't connecting the dots.

From here, Rice continued with the story.

"After the war against the monsters was over, Bal shifted his focus to other endeavours. He always wanted to solve life's ultimate challenge, death. So he studied and did research, and what he found was forbidden magic that has been banished for millennia, Necromancy.

Many mages were not fond of his ideas but he had some followers. I wanted to keep a close eye on him, so I stayed near his group. One day, he attempted to perform the ritual with his followers but something went terribly wrong. All his followers were sacrificed in the process. Only he and I survived.

We were cursed with immortality that day.

With all that time, he lived through the decline of the mages. Slowly, they lost their influence in Diamondvania and their numbers dwindled. It drove him mad, and he wanted revenge by reopening that portal and unleashing the nightmare from centuries ago."

"We have to stop him!" Olivia called out.

"Good idea, only one problem." Ehsaas threw out.

"What's that?" The Summoner asked.

"The guy is immortal, remember?" Ehsaas replied.

Afomia turned to Rice. "Is there any way to stop him?"

"I've tried many times before but failed." Rice admitted.

Afomia and Olivia both looked down. They were struggling to figure out a way to save their friend. Seeing that they were making no progress, Ehsaas spoke up.

"Let's all get some rest."

"What?! You are just going to give up like that?!" Afomia was angry.

"We need a fresh mind. Staying up won't do us any good."

"They boy has a point." Rice affirmed.

"Alright, then it's settled. We'll get some rest and think of a way to save Saanjh tomorrow." Olivia announced to the group.

They all left the seating area within the cave and found separate spots to rest for the night. Although they were all quiet and lying down, they all continued swimming in their thoughts for a bit longer before falling asleep.

SAANJH SLOWLY OPENED her eyes and her mind slowly adjusted to her being conscious again. She found herself in a dark cellar of sorts encased within a magical barrier. It was similar to the one at the hidden basement, only this one felt even stronger. Regardless, Saanjh was about to attempt to shatter the veil, but she was interrupted by a stranger she didn't notice.

"It's no use." Saanjh was startled by the girl's presence. She looked as if she could be Saanjh's age.

"Don't say that. There is a way out of everything." The Mage said.

"It's an anti-magical barrier. We are magicians who rely solely on magic. Therefore, we cannot break ourselves out. Someone from the outside needs to come save us."

"Ha, well you are in luck, because I know some people who are on their way to rescue us."

"The girl paused for a moment before speaking to Saanjh again. "Can I ask you something?"

"What is it?" Saanjh focussed on the other girl.

"The people on their way, are they strong enough to defeat the one who put us here?" The other girl asked quietly.

Saanjh hesitated and lost her ability to speak temporarily. She tried to form words but they never materialized.

"I see... Then for the sake of your friends, I hope they don't come." The girl said sadly.

She turned away and continued to sit, leaning against the wall. In contrast, Saanjh stood still, thinking about every word she had just heard. Her mind began to spiral into negativity, seeing her friends all fall to the Necromancer.

Chapter 15: Mage Arianna

After resting to recuperate his energy, Ehsaas was attempting to figure out where Saanjh had been taken. He used the rocks and sticks he had found to help him visualize and think of possibilities of where the enemy's lair could be. Was the enemy hiding within the village like the vampires and werewolves? He didn't think that was likely.

Or maybe he was hidden in a cave similar to where Ehsaas was now. There were too many things to consider and Ehsaas couldn't pinpoint an approximate location. He grew so frustrated that he picked up one of the rocks cracking it as he threw it against the cavern wall.

That was the action that triggered something within Ehsaas's mind. Something that had been disturbing him was why the Necromancer abducted Saanjh and not Afomia nor Olivia. In terms of power and skill, the other two were better options. Then, it clicked in his mind.

"Oh no... We have to save Saanjh now!" He yelled.

AFOMIA HAD WOKEN UP earlier but still feeling tired, she continued to lay down and rest her eyes. In doing so, her mind began to wander and images of the marks on the Necromancer's body began floating in her mind.

"Where have I seen those before?" She asked herself.

Suddenly those marks began to glow and create a blinding flash in Afomia's mind. Although it was her thought, the image felt so real. It made her jump back to reality where she stood on her feet.

"I know where they took Saanjh." She said aloud.

OLIVIA FOUND A PLACE within the cavern where she could be alone. She held out the stone that used to contain her eagle. Gripping the stone tight to her chest, she began thinking about how she wouldn't stand any chance against the necromancer if they were to battle again.

She searched for answers in her thoughts, which led her to only one possible outcome. It was something passed down to her from many generations of summoner's past. She began to hear the voice of one of her elders.

"Olivia, you are a kind person. Therefore, what I'm about to show you, I hope you never have to call upon."

Once she finished listening to her memory, Olivia took her stance and a deep breath. Her hands were ready to move and she was focusing her energy to conjure something powerful. She was about to begin her incantation, but she was interrupted by a pebble hitting her head. She opened her eyes to see it was Rice.

"What's with the goofy stance?" He pointed out.

"Argh! I was in the middle of my training!"

Annoyed, Olivia attempted to strike him. She threw a punch but he suddenly disappeared.

"What the? Where did he...?"

"Over here!" Rice jested.

He appeared a few meters to her right. Infuriated by his taunt. She attempted a second attack, only to have her momentum be used against her as she tripped. Her face would have smashed against the ground but Rice pulled her by the arm and brought her back, standing.

After the scuffle, Olivia calmed down and stopped. She could see Rice had his back facing her as he had something important to say.

"We haven't exhausted all our options yet. So there is no need to go playing the heroine."

Olivia remained silent, allowing his words to sink into her mind. She looked at all the summoning stones she still had, and it made her realize how much she still had to live for. The summoner was about to thank Rice but arriving at the scene was the detective.

"Ehsaas! How was your..." Olivia started.

"No time for that, I've figured out why Bal kidnapped Saanjh. We have to find her now!" He said urgently.

"But we still have no idea where she is being kept."

"I know." Afomia had just appeared.

"Where are they?" Ehsaas pressed.

"In the cabin hidden in the woods." the Templar replied.

"What would some old necromancer be doing in a place like that?" Olivia wondered.

"I'll explain on the way, but I hope I'm wrong." Afomia responded with urgency.

Ehsaas and Olivia left quickly to prepare what they needed before storming Bal's lair. Afomia was about to do the same but Rice held her back.

"Hey, we can't waste anymore time, Saanjh is in danger." Afomia tried to get past him.

"I know, but there is something I must tell you that you can't tell the others." Rice had an intense look on his face.

Afomia had a feeling this was very serious. "What did you need to tell me?"

"I'm going to tell you how to defeat Bal."

Her eyes were wide open and she listened closely to every word he had to say.

MUCH TIME HAD PASSED but without any sign of daylight, it was impossible to tell exactly how long Saanjh had been trapped for. However, that did not deter her spirit. She continuously attempted to break the anti-magic barrier, but she could barely conjure any of her spells correctly.

"Argh! Fire, water, ice, lightning. Why doesn't any of my spells work?!" Her frustration was obvious.

"Maybe because you don't have an affinity for that magic." Replied the girl with a timid voice.

"Wait what? What do you mean?" Saanjh asked.

"Well you see, every magician has a type of magic that is most natural to them. It is only after a magician becomes proficient with their element that they can move onto others."

"So you are saying the reason I'm having trouble with all those spells isn't because I'm an incompetent mage, but because I haven't figured out my signature magic?

The other mage nodded slowly and was suddenly met with a massive embrace from Saanjh. The timid magician was confused but attempted to comfort Saanjh who was crying.

"Umm, is everything okay?"

Saanjh took a moment before speaking again. "For so long I thought I was a failure because I couldn't cast a single spell properly. Thank you so much for telling me that."

"It's nothing. I only told you what I know." The small girl said quietly.

"What's your name?" Saanjh asked, wiping away her tears.

"Arianna."

"Mine's Saanjh. So how does a magician figure out their affinity?"

"I don't know how to answer that." The soft spoken mage replied.

"Arianna please, I need to know!"

"No seriously, I don't know. Most magicians usually discover their affinity at a young age. They wouldn't even have much recollection of how they figured it out."

Saanjh felt discouraged again, but then she grew curious. "So, what's yours?"

"Mine? It's, umm..." She was very hesitant to share but then a voice appeared in the room. One that sent shivers down the spines of most people.

"Support magic. The weakest kind there is." The voice said harshly.

It was none other than Bal. His presence was frightening Arianna and his comment disheartened her. However, Saanjh would not stand for it.

"How could you say that about her? Arianna is very knowledgeable about magic!" She shouted.

"Tch, what good does knowledge do without application?"

"Arianna is still young, she has the potential to be..." Saanjh felt Arianna's hand pulling on her arm.

"Hey, it's okay." Arianna whispered.

"No it's not! Don't take this garbage from him!" Saanjh continued to raise her voice.

"Hahahahah! See what I mean? Not only does she have the weakest affinity, but the girl lacks any sense of fighting instinct."

"I'll show you fighting instinct!" Saanjh leapt up on her feet and attempted to blast Bal with a spell. However, her magic failed, leaving her feeling embarrassed.

"A failure of a magician along with a mage with a useless affinity. Absolutely pathetic." Bal said with contempt.

The Necromancer turned his back on the two mages, left the room and slammed the door. He walked past two skeletal brutes that stood guard even after he left the prison.

After seeing the door closed, Saanjh turned to Arianna. "Pay no attention to him, he doesn't know what he is talking ..."

"He's right."

"Wait, what?" Saanjh stammered.

"My magic is very weak and won't be much help in breaking us out of here." Arianna said miserably.

"Arianna, don't say that. I'm sure there is a way to..."

"But you can." Arianna's tone changed in an instant.

Saanjh was shocked by what she had just heard. Arianna had been timid this whole time until those words left her mouth. Something about her was different.

"Me? What can I do?" Saanjh was a bit confused.

"I think I know what your affinity is." Arianna retorted.

"You do?! What is it? Tell me quickly!"

"Well, if my hunch is correct, then you possess the chaos attribute."

"Chaos? What is that? How do you even know?" Saanjh questioned.

"From what I've learned, it's nearly impossible for a magician to cast a spell outside of their affinity, even with full mastery of their own. The fact that you can even generate a hint of fire, lightning, ice, and water, leads me to believe that you are a chaos mage. You have the ability to make combinations of different elements. The drawback is that it's extremely risky and random."

"Could you teach me how?" Saanjh was pleading with the other mage.

"Well, I can't cast your type of spells. However, the principles should still be the same. I'll show you the basics with my technique if that will help."

"It would be an honour." Saanjh was elated.

Chapter 16: Blood Moon

On this night, there was a radiant blood moon in the sky. This was the opportunity the werewolves had been waiting for. Chef Lycan had his forces assembled, standing in the forest where they saw a tall stony tower. Within that structure was their greatest enemy.

There was a moment of silence, before a loud howl could be heard throughout the woods. That was the signal for the army of werewolves to lay siege on the vampires' tower.

The Count's minions were in a panic after hearing the howl. They began mustering as many of their forces as possible to defend their base.

The wolves were relentless in their assault. With the extra boost in power they received from the full moon, the vampire minions stood no chance. The vampire army was forced to retreat while the wolves pressed their advantage.

Chef Lycan could smell victory was within his grasp, but he also caught the scent of someone familiar nearby. He ordered the majority of his forces to continue the onslaught while he went with a small squad to attend to another matter.

In the distance, Olivia, Ehsaas, Afomia, and Rice were making haste towards the cabin. They could hear the fighting from afar but remained focussed on their current path. It seemed they weren't going to run into much interference, until a pack of wolves lept out from the bushes, attempting to ambush the group.

Olivia, Ehsaas, and Afomia were caught off guard and couldn't react in time. Intercepting the pre-emptive strike was Rice, who appeared in front of them. He clapped the ground with his hands and a shockwave was created, sending the werewolves flying and landing on their backs.

As those werewolves were shaking off the hit, a couple more appeared from the trees. Olivia, Ehsaas, and Afomia were ready to fight, but Rice advised against it.

"I'll hold them off. The three of you, go find Bal and rescue Saanjh!" He instructed them.

The three fighters reluctantly obeyed, continuing to run towards the cabin. The werewolves attempted to follow, but Rice casted a fire wall to hinder their movement. He stayed to ensure none of them would get past him.

Afomia continued to lead the way towards Bal's lair. Ehsaas was second, followed by Olivia, who caught wind that they were being tracked. She attempted to alert her allies but something ran at a rapid speed, passing her. It appeared still behind Afomia, but catching up to Ehsaas.

It was Chef Lycan, who was about to swing his claw at the Detective. Afomia shouted for Ehsaas to move but he couldn't reach in time. Instead, it was Olivia's wolf that jumped in to bite Lycan's arm, forcing him to miss his attack.

Olivia stood next to her wolf, ready to fight the werewolf leader but Afomia stepped in. "You go on ahead." She ordered.

"What? But only you know the way to..."

"Your wolf can track him down. Just give her the scent and you'll find him."

Olivia felt torn as she wanted to help her friends fight but Afomia assured her. "I know you want a rematch against that necromancer."

"Hah, you bet I do." Olivia said and thanked Afomia before pulling out one of Max's feathers that had the scent of the Necromancer on it. Once Saanvi took a sniff of the feather, the scent was identified and she led the way. That left Afomia and Ehsaas to face off against the alpha of the pack.

Ehsaas fired a silver bolt without warning, but Lycan's speed was at its peak. Not only did the arrow miss, but the werewolf appeared behind the detective, who never saw his enemy's movement. Afomia attempted to swing her spear at her target, but with a swift swipe of his claws, the Holy Knight lost her weapon and she fell to the ground landing on one knee. Ehsaas attempted to fire another arrow, but the werewolf swatted away the crossbow and kicked the detective in the gut.

Both Afomia and Ehsaas were near each other, struggling to stand.

"His speed is too much, we can't keep up." Afomia pointed out.

"I know, we won't last much longer at this rate." Ehsaas agreed.

"How disappointing. I was expecting more from our rematch, Detective, but I guess this is the end." The werewolf's snarl turned into a grin.

Lycan was ready to devour the two fighters, starting with Ehsaas. As the werewolf stood tall with his arms stretched, they could see his shadow expand on the ground. However, there was something usual about the shadow, as something began to emerge from it. Manifesting behind Lycan was the Lord of Vampires.

"What?! How did you get here?!" Lycan's growl sounded nervous.

"It's a neat little trick I picked up from the magicians." Responded the Count.

"Tch, it matters not, it's a full blood moon and I'm far more powerful than..." The leader of the werewolves suddenly stopped when he felt a bit weaker. "What did you do to me?"

"You didn't think I knew about the moon tonight?" The vampire asked with a devious smile.

Lycan finally realized that he had fallen for the Count's trap. The Lord of Vampires left his tower's defenses weak on purpose, luring the werewolves in. Worse of all, Chef Lycan decided to split up his forces. While all this was happening, the Count hid under Lycan's shadow, casting an energy drain ability.

Now that the ability was fully activated, not only was Lycan's energy siphoned, but his body deteriorated into a lifeless colour. When it was complete, the Alpha's body faded to dust.

"Farewell, old friend." The Count felt a hint of remorse but only briefly.

The Vampire held some of the dust in his hand before allowing it to blow away with the wind. He then summoned one of his loyal bat minions that appeared before him.

"Commence the counterattack." He ordered.

The bat flew up and let out a screech through the forest. A mass of the vampire army appeared out of hiding and the werewolves were now trapped within the tower. There was no escape as the tide of battle had shifted.

Chapter 17: Chaos Magic

Still trapped within the barrier, Saanjh was focusing on her magic. On one hand, she was able to conjure a flame and on the other, a water orb. She was doing her best to maintain the two elements for as long as possible.

"Almost there, you're doing great. Keep holding it..." Arianna encouraged her.

Shortly after, Saanjh finally gave out. "How long was that?"

"About ten minutes." The other mage replied.

"Wow, really?" Saanjh felt a little proud.

"Yeah!" Arianna agreed. "You have improved so much in such a short span of time!"

"Well, I have a great teacher." Saanjh said with a smile.

They were about to do another training session until they heard the prison door opening. The girls immediately stopped all their activity, as a giant skeleton guard entered. The barrier suddenly disappeared, leaving both of the magicians confused. They were grabbed by the brute, Saanjh on its right arm and Arianna on its left. Then, they were carried out of the prison. Arianna didn't move much, but Saanjh kept struggling to break free.

"Hey, stop squirming." Arianna whispered.

"What? No way! We are done for if we don't escape now!" Saanjh continued to struggle.

"I don't think so. If he wanted to get rid of us, he would have done it a long time ago. He clearly needs us for something."

"What would he possibly want from us?"

"I don't know. Just save your energy, and maybe we'll find out." Arianna suggested.

"Hmph, fine." Saanjh wasn't happy, but she agreed to stop for the time being.

After a few more steps, the brute dropped both of the magicians on the ground.

"Ow! You could have put us down gently!" Saanjh felt a bit of pain on her lower back. She then looked to Arianna who was quiet, with a frightened look on her face. Saanjh followed Arianna's eyes and saw the circle with red paint marking in the middle of the basement.

"This place, again..." The words just left her lips as Saanjh recognized the place from before, when she was with Afomia. Only this time, the candles were lit and a ritual was ready to be performed.

"Welcome!" Bal's voice caught their attention. "You two have the special opportunity to help restore honour to the race of the magicians!" He bellowed.

"And how exactly are you going to do that?" Saanjh questioned.

Bal walked closer to the circle before speaking. "Locked away within this portal are hidden horrors that have not walked these lands for centuries. You two are going to help me release them.

"Pft, as if. Why would we ever help you do that?" Saanjh laughed at the idea.

"He's using us as a sacrifice." Arianna felt her stomach drop as she realized.

"What?! Ain't no way am I ending up as food for some monster portal!" Saanjh yelled as she went into her fighting stance. The skeletal brute was about to intervene but its master held it back.

"This won't take long." Bal remarked.

The Necromancer was expecting Saanjh to be nothing but a warm-up. Saanjh threw a fireball and Bal held his hand out, thinking it would be a weak spell.

"This again? If it didn't work the first time, then it definitely won't..." Bal was initially expecting a weak attempt.

Suddenly the fireball burst into freezing fire shards. Bal had to react quickly, casting a shield that would negate most of the attack. However, a shard slipped through and cut a part of his robe near his chest. He was surprised by the result of Saanjh's attack.

"What's wrong? You look a bit nervous there." Saanjh taunted.

"Lucky shot, it won't happen again." He gritted his teeth.

He pointed to his skeletal brute and then casted a spell that disassembled his own loyal guard. Bal then lifted his hands and the bones began to float around and reassemble into different entities. Instead of just one brute, there were now five smaller but much more versatile skeleton warriors at his command. Their order was to deal with the annoying magician.

Seeing her new foes, Saanjh attempted to use her freeze-fire ability again. The shards hit against her enemies but they didn't seem fazed by her attacks. It was as if they had no comprehension of pain. Saanjh grew nervous as she had nowhere to run, so she looked around, spotting Arianna close by. The sight of her friend sparked a conversation they had during their training. She decided to give the technique a try.

"Channel your energy to the center of your body. Relax your breathing and maintain it once you find that perfect rhythm." Saanjh was hearing Arianna's voice from her memories.

The skeleton warriors were marching closer as Saanjh continued to maintain her current state. She remained still until she felt a sudden surge of electrical energy. At that moment, she opened her eyes wide, but they were glowing white, and her pupils could not be seen. The skeletons halted their advance as the Magician spread out her arms.

They waited, and in a blink of an eye, a lightning bolt fuelled by chaotic energy struck one of the minions and then chained to another. Despite being struck, they were able to reassemble themselves. However, more and more chaotic bolts appeared, striking anything without warning. Not only were Bal's summons shattered to pieces, but he had to cast a higher level barrier to ensure his own safety.

After defending himself, he looked for the caster, seeking revenge, but she was already lying on the ground unconscious. Saanjh hadn't learned how to control the immense power of chaos magic, and was struck by her own attack. Her eyes were closed as Arianna sat beside her. Seeing this, Bal walked up to the magicians and spoke to the one still conscious.

"Not bad, she improved significantly. I'm guessing you have something to do with that."

Arianna nervously nodded. Bal also noticed that Saanjh's injuries had been mitigated because Arianna casted a shield at the last moment before the chaotic bolt struck Saanjh. He used his telekinetic ability to move Saanjh away from Arianna then he put the support magician inside a prison.

Bal then held his hand over Saanjh's body, preparing to cast a spell on her. A dark red circle began to form around the unconscious spellcaster. Arianna yelled as she slammed the magical forcefield.

"Stop! Please don't sacrifice her!" She begged.

"Don't worry, I've had a change of heart. She has proven to be of greater use than I initially thought." Bal replied maliciously.

Suddenly, the space around Saanjh turned to black. A dark shadow appeared and wrapped itself around Saanjh, engulfing her entire body. Arianna could only watch in her horror as her friend was beginning to fade away.

Chapter 18: Lord of Vampires

After absorbing his arch nemesis' powers, the Lord of Vampires stood revelling over his assured victory. He decided to display some of his new abilities by having two large wings appear from his back shoulders. As he spread his wings out, he dashed towards the detective and the holy knight striking them both simultaneously. They were sent back quite the distance but were surprisingly still able to stand after taking such a hit.

"How are you holding up?" Afomia asked.

"Been better. But I've also felt worse." Ehsaas replied.

"I've never faced anything this powerful before." The Templar replied.

"Neither have I, but I think there is a way to beat him." There was some optimism in the archer's voice.

"What? How are we going to do that? We couldn't even handle the leader of the werewolves and this guy is at least twice as strong."

"True, but he's much slower." Ehsaas pointed out.

Him saying so, restored Afomia's hope. "How long can you keep him distracted?" She asked.

"Three minutes? Four tops."

"Can you make it five?" Afomia bargained.

"That extra minute is going to feel like an eternity." Ehsaas did not sound pleased.

"I'll buy lunch for the entire week." The Templar offered.

"Make it lunch and dinner, then we have a deal."

"Well you gotta make it happen first."

"Oh I will. Better get the money ready!" Ehsaas called out as he moved towards the Vampire Lord with haste and Afomia drove her spear into the ground. Then the Templar sat down, put her hands on her knees and began her meditation.

The Count noticed Ehsaas firing silver bolts in his direction. To counter, the vampire hardened his wings to stone and nullified the arrows fired by the Detective. Then, with the swing of one of his wings, blood shards were released, which Ehsaas dodged. Not wanting to give his enemy a chance to react, the hunter aimed his bow to where he thought the vampire would be, but his target had disappeared.

Using a dark veil ability, the Count made himself invisible to the human eyes. Ehsaas reached for some dust in his pouch and began throwing it into the air, scattering it throughout the open space in the forest.

As the particles dropped, some of it landed on the Count, giving away his position. The Detective now had his bow aimed at his target, but the vampire's speed allowed it to appear in front of Ehsaas. The Hunter's crossbow was slapped away from his hands by the wings of the vampire.

"A valiant effort, but cheap tricks can never compensate for real power. Any last words?" The Vampire Lord taunted.

"Yeah, just letting you know, that stuff isn't dust. It's powder."

Ehsaas jumped back and threw a lit match he had covered from the vampire's line of sight. When the fire made contact with the powder, an explosion occurred between the two combatants. Flames spread at an alarming speed, too quick for even the Vampire Lord to overrun.

"Ahhhhhh!" The Count screamed.

The grotesque mutant was flailing around with fire over his body, yelling in pain. This was the first time Ehsaas had seen the powerful dark lord in such a state. He realized this might be his only chance. He picked up his crossbow and lined it up with the vampire's heart. He took a deep breath then fired the shot.

Jumping in front was one of the loyal minions of the Vampire Lord, the Humbat. It slashed the arrow away and then swung its wing, knocking Ehsaas to the ground. The Humbat was about to strike his defenseless opponent, as Ehsaas braced himself for the worst.

DEEP WITHIN AFOMIA'S mind, she found herself in a tranquil and peaceful place. It reminded her much of the monastery, where she trained and grew up. The only difference was that there seemed to be no one around.

"Hello?" Her voice echoed through the halls but there was no reply, so she wandered through the building, seeking for answers.

After what seemed like hours, Afomia still found herself walking through the entire building. She found it quite strange, as she didn't remember the monastery being quite so massive. It was from that thought, that she decided to hit one of the columns with her spear. With a mark left on the structural beam, she continued to walk again.

Similar to before, Afomia ventured through the sanctuary and still no one to be found. In addition to that, she looked around to find the column with the exact same marking that she had made earlier with her spear. This confirmed her suspicion, she had been walking around in circles.

"Alright, enough games. Show yourself." She called out to the entire temple. Initially, there wasn't a reply, but Afomia waited and then, a voice appeared.

"Well done. You definitely possess patience, one of the virtues required to be a true templar knight." Eventually, the voice manifested into a human figure, one that had Afomia in shock.

"Master... Master Ruthar!"

"I'm a spirit avatar within you and I take the form of someone you have a close friendship with."

"How fitting. Master Ruthar has taught me pretty much everything I know."

"Now, what is it you seek?" The Spirit Avatar inquired.

"My friends are in danger. I need to unlock the full power of a holy templar. Please, will you help me?"

"I cannot help one who lacks all the necessary qualities of a templar. So tell me, do you have everything it takes to become one of the holy templars?"

"I do." She said with full confidence.

The spirit, impersonating Afomia's master, walked up to her and quickly assessed her. "Intriguing. You possess courage, patience, discipline, strength, and character. Indeed you have many of the qualities needed to become a holy templar. However, there is one thing you lack, or rather, you need to let go of."

"And what is that?"

"Your human emotions." The Spirit replied.

Afomia took a deep breath before replying. "Okay, I'm ..." She paused when the spirit began changing forms rapidly. It was transforming through everyone in Afomia's life. Her family members and her friends. The sight of their faces put her in silence.

"What's wrong? Not so easy is it? Guess you don't have what it takes." The spirit began to walk away, but then it stopped."

"No! I can do this! I need to do this! In order to save Ehsaas, Saanjh, Olivia, and everyone!"

"Very well, let's see if your mind can survive the process."

The spirit placed its hand on her head and a radiant force rushed through Afomia's entire body. It was known as the purification ritual for one to transcend into a templar knight. For a moment, all her memories were flashing before her eyes, it was not something a normal human could handle. She yelled in pain but no one could hear her, as her body became numb and the light was taking over her mind.

Returning back to the forest, Ehsaas was vulnerable to the Humbat that was about to strike him down. It raised its claws but before it could land the attack, it felt a weird sensation around its chest. Looking down, it saw that a spear of light had pierced through its body. The Humbat faded to dust, revealing Afomia as the wielder of the radiant spear.

More of the vampire minions flooded in, ready to attack. Afomia stood surrounded by an aura of light. With one swing of her spear, she created a wave of light that obliterated half of the forces that attempted to swarm her. The remaining half were quivering in fear after what they had just witnessed. Even Ehsaas, who was saved by Afomia, had doubts about what his friend had become. There were no longer pupils in her eyes, as they were glowing with light.

"Afomia? Is that you?" He called out.

"Hmmm? Oh you must be referring to my former identity. I am now a transcendent templar knight." Her voice had changed. It was slightly lower pitched and had somewhat of an echo.

"Okay... Then what should I call you?" Ehsaas asked.

"There is no need to be concerned about names. I have only one mission and that is to eliminate all that defiles the templar order."

She swung her spear again, taking out another vampire minion. There was a clear difference in their strength and all the vampire underlings could sense it. Instead of standing to fight, they attempted to flee.

The Templar Knight was not amused by their cowardice. She was ready to hunt them all down but she never got the chance. The vampire creatures all stood still for a moment before having their essences drawn out of their bodies. Every single one that was left, got absorbed into the Count, who held out his hand.

"Ahh, a holy templar. It's been quite some time since I fought against one of your kind. Tell me, how does it feel knowing I nearly destroyed your entire race?" He directed his comment at Afomia.

"Us templars have no need for petty vengeance." Afomia replied in a mono-toned voice.

"Ha, we'll see about that!" The Vampire Lord said as he launched a swarm of vicious bats at Afomia, who stood defiantly. As the fangs were about to reach her, she wheeled her spear, creating a spinning light shield that vapourized the bats that made contact against it.

The Count realized this wasn't going to be a free victory, but he was more than certain that he would prevail as the victor. He was preparing to cast a stronger spell but a veil was suddenly created, separating the Vampire Lord from Ehsaas and Afomia. The one who casted the barrier was Rice, who had trapped himself inside with the dark foe.

"Go help Olivia." He struggled to speak as he was holding the barrier.

Ehsaas wasted no time arguing and immediately got up. In contrast, Afomia remained for a moment.

"Is that you Afomia?" Rice asked.

"Afomia is no more." The Knight replied.

"Figures. Well, you better get going. You are obligated to fulfill Afomia's wishes after all."

"Don't get too comfortable. I will return to cleanse the world from your presence."

"I guess the Holy Templars aren't too happy with me, huh?" Rice teased.

The Holy Templar didn't bother to reply. Tired of his presence, she left with Ehsaas to find Olivia and Saanjh. That left Rice alone with the Lord of Vampires.

"I see you were able to handle those wolves with ease." The Count complimented.

"Actually, you weakened them quite a bit, after taking out their leader. Guess I should thank you for that."

"Ha, don't expect any more favours from here."

"Do your worst." Rice challenged.

Chapter 19: Soul-bond

Powerful clashes between the elder mage and Vampire Lord were creating shockwaves that could be felt from miles away. It was truly a battle between two titans. Ehsaas couldn't believe he was fighting against one of those beings not too long ago. He was thankful he somehow managed to stay alive despite his injuries. Now, his mission was to find Olivia, and help her in getting Saanjh back.

"Hey you." Ehsaas was directing his comment to the spirit that had taken over Afomia's body.

"What is it, human?"

"I've read about a templar knight taking a transcendent form. I'm guessing you fit that description." Ehsaas started.

"That is correct."

Continuing, Ehsaas said, "I also read that although you don't take the identity of the body you inhabit, you do retain their memories. Am I correct?"

"Hmm, for a human, you possess quite the knowledge. What is it you are getting at?" The Templar's interest was piqued.

"I overheard a conversation Afomia had with that mage who's battling the Vampire Lord. He mentioned he knew how to defeat Bal the Necromancer, who is behind all this. Do you have any recollection of that?"

"And what if I do?" Replied the Templar Knight.

"Then my only question is, will you be able to complete the task?"

"Why do you ask such a question? Do you doubt a transcendent being's power?" Her tone grew more aggressive.

"No. I just know if it were up to Afomia, she probably wouldn't be able to do it. She's far too kind." Ehsaas looked down to the ground as he spoke.

"Fear not. I won't be hindered by emotions."

"Good, because if you can't do it, then I will." Ehsaas said determined.

SAANVI CONTINUED TO lead the way with Olivia following behind. They were making great pace until Saanvi stopped. She had picked up a different scent, leaving Olivia confused.

"What is it, Saanvi?"

Stepping out from behind one of the trees was a hooded, cloaked figure shrouded with a dark aura. Olivia couldn't see the person's face but she didn't need to. She had felt this aura before and there was only one person who could possess such a presence.

"Bal!" Olivia commanded her companion to attack but the wolf did not obey. "Saanvi, what's wrong?" The wolf had no intent to fight as it walked behind her summoner. Thinking Saanvi was too afraid to face Bal, Olivia recalled her back into her summoning stone and deferred to her other companions.

Nicholas, the rhino was summoned to the fray. He stomped the ground before charging at the sorcerer at full speed.

"Iron hide ability, activate!" Olivia shouted and the rhino's skin became tougher than stone.

The Mage standing on the opposing side began to cast a spell. Above the figure's head, a dark fiery mist began swirling. Olivia thought this was the attack but instead, all that came out of the smoke was the number '2'.

A chaotic energy blast blindsided Nicholas and struck him in the face. Initially, it seemed to have no effect, until the rhino slowly stopped running. The companion's mind had been affected and its perception had been altered. Nicholas began seeing horrific nightmares within his brain. In reality, his body had gone into a seizure, rendering him unable to defend himself.

The Mage followed up by casting another spell, this time the number '7' appeared in the mist. A chaos bolt randomly occurred and critically struck the rhino, leaving him unable to battle. The sorcerer saw his chance to dispose of the beast, but Olivia reacted quickly and managed to recall her companion before he took a fatal hit.

The Summoner was now furious and had to resort to calling out her next ally. This one required four summoning stones and appearing on the battlefield was a spirit lion, letting out a ferocious roar. His name was Attis.

Despite seeing a new foe, the Magician failed to see how this one was any different from the rhino or the wolf. Again, the dark mage's ability was used, this time, the number '6' appeared and emerging from the ground was a terrifying chaos creature holding a scythe. In addition, a spiritual chain was attached to the spawn's chest, linking it to the mage's heart.

Having studied about the vast range of summons, Olivia knew what kind of opponent she was up against. This was an incredibly powerful creature that came at a cost, part of the summoner's life.

The Spirit Lion pounced at his foe, while the chaos summon retaliated with its scythe. They exchanged slashes against one another and looked fairly even at first. However, as the battle wore on, the chaos fiend drained part of its owner's life force. With the extra power boost, it launched a chaos energy beam from the swing of its weapon. Attis attempted to dodge it, but the width of the beam caught his leg.

Although it was only a minor injury, the lion's movement got significantly slower. With each swing, Attis was being overpowered by the monster. Having witnessed enough, Olivia called upon a unique summoner technique.

"Soul-bond!" She called out.

This was an ability that allowed the lion's soul to merge with Olivia's body. Suddenly, her body was wrapped with a spiritual armour. Her hands were replaced with spirit claws and she possessed the strength and tenacity of a lion.

The chaos fiend was not impressed thinking Olivia had only undergone a change on the surface. So it swung its weapon where she stood, but its blade was stopped by Olivia's lion claw. The monster was stunned and it couldn't react when Olivia counterattacked with her other arm and slashed at her opponent.

Not wanting to lose composure, the fiend stole more life from its summoner. Feeling reinvigorated, it charged full force at Olivia. However, she slipped past its attack, completely ignoring it. The creature was confused until it realized that its body wasn't the target. Olivia was successful in breaking off the chain.

Without any sustenance, the chaos summon was withering away. It attempted one last desperate swing at its foe. The scythe was about an inch from Olivia's nose but that was as close as it would get. The essence of the fiend scattered and all that was left was the spellcaster who summoned it.

Not wanting to give her enemy a chance to recover, Olivia slashed her new target. However, the Mage just avoided a clean cut to the face.

"Lucky dodge. You won't be able to do that again." The Summoner pointed out.

Olivia increased her speed and kicked her enemy, knocking the caster's head against the ground. Because of the impact, Olivia foe was now unconscious, presenting her with the opportunity to put an end to this battle. Yet, before she could land her attack, a shield appeared around the mage.

The shield was easily shattered by Olivia's spirit lion claw, but that was enough time for someone to step in front of the summoner's enemy. It was Arianna.

"I don't know who you are, but step aside if you value your life." Arianna did not budge. "Then you leave me no choice."

Olivia was about to swing the spirit claws but Arianna casted another defensive shield. This one was able to withstand Olivia's first strike but she continued swinging. With each hit, the cracks on the barrier got larger.

"Fortify!" The support mage shouted.

Immediately after the second forcefield shattered, Arianna created a third barrier. Olivia was getting annoyed but she could tell the support mage wasn't going to last much longer. Sweat was dripping from Arianna's forehead and she was breathing heavily. It would only take a few more slashes and the support mage would probably give out.

"I don't know why you are protecting that evil necromancer, but if I have to take you out to get to him, then so be it."

Olivia had both her claws in the air and was ready for the final strike.

Arianna was bracing herself for the worse until she processed what the Summoner had said. "Necromancer? Wait, you must think... No, stop! That's not Ba..."

Before Arianna could finish her sentence, Olivia's attack connected against the barrier fracturing it to pieces. In addition, the impact was so great, it sent Arianna slamming onto the ground.

The sound of Arianna's defeat alerted the unconscious mage. Part of the magician's face was now revealed, looking up to see what caused the commotion. To Olivia's dismay, it was not someone she was expecting.

"No, it can't be... Saanjh?!"

The chaos mage's mind was not fully coherent. She seemed disoriented, not even sure of her own identity. First, she stared at the summoner. Although it was faint, a small memory appeared in her mind briefly.

"Olivia? Who? I...?" Saanjh stammered.

Her eyes moved and was now fixated on the unconscious support mage. The sight of seeing Arianna injured triggered a spell that was lying dormant within Saanjh. Suddenly, a burst of negative energy flowed out of Saanjh's body. Her eyes had turned ominous red as she let out a horrifying shriek.

Seeing her friend in distress, Olivia began walking towards Saanjh, hoping to calm her down. Unfortunately, the chaos magician had no control over her body. A massive burst of chaotic energy shot out directly at the summoner. Olivia had to react quickly, attempting to block the surge of magic with her lion claws. They were able to prevent her from sustaining a major injury but Olivia's spirit armour was beginning to shatter.

First, the armour on her torso was withering away, and there was only a fraction of spirit energy left on the two lion claws. Olivia was exhausted, barely able to stand up while breathing heavily. In contrast, her opponent was filled with uncontrollable chaos energy.

"Saanjh, I can't believe you've become this strong." Olivia said in almost a whisper.

There were no words returning from the mage's mouth, only a terrifying shriek. When she finished, she began making her way towards the Summoner.

"Looks like this is it. I'm sorry for not being able to save you Saanjh." Olivia closed her eyes.

As a swirl of negative energy was beginning to engulf Olivia, Saanvi forced her way out of her summoning stone. The loyal spirit wolf had materialized to defend her caretaker. She stood firm with her teeth out, growling at her enemy.

Opening her eyes again, Olivia said, "Saanvi, what are you doing? I thought you didn't want to fight."

It was when she finished her sentence that Olivia realized why Saanvi didn't listen to her initially. Saanvi knew all along they were about to fight Saanjh, because she recognized the mage's scent.

However, Saanvi no longer had a choice now that her summoner's life was in danger. Not wanting to waste time, Saanvi attempted to strike first by jumping into the air.

"No Saanvi, she's too power..." The Summoner struggled to finish.

Olivia's warning was too late, as Saanjh randomly casted a spell that pushed the wolf back. Thankfully, Saanvi was able to shake off the attack. Knowing her strength alone wouldn't be enough, something within the wolf caused it to gain a new power. The marks on her body began to glow and she let out a howl that could be heard from miles away.

From the howl, two more spirit wolves emerged beside Saanvi. Then, at the palm of Olivia's hand, the summoning stones for the two new companions, materialized. Their names were engraved on the stones, Meisha and Jasreen.

The three spirit wolves fought as a pack and strategically combated their enemy. They attacked from different angles at different times to throw off Saanjh's rhythm. Their tactic was working, as the mage couldn't focus on any one target. Unfortunately, the wolves' attack would not be enough to take down the sorceress.

Each hit was only magnifying her rage, and the madness spell that was casted on Saanjh made her go berserk. A random spell was chosen, this one being a nova pulse that unleashed around her. Saanvi, Jasreen, and Meisha were all caught in mid-jump and struck to the ground. None of them were able to continue battling after such a powerful blast.

Olivia was now experiencing traumatic flashbacks with what happened to Max. She had a feeling history was about to repeat itself. Sensing this, Olivia was ready to pull out her last resort. She took a deep breath, readying her hands to perform a complex summoning ritual.

As she spoke the first word, a wave of light appeared between the spirit wolves and Saanjh. The enraged magician was forced to jump away as the light energy caused her pain. She then looked to see who interrupted her, and it was none other than the Holy Templar.

Chapter 20: Former Friends

The Mage of chaos stood on one side while the Holy Templar was on the opposite. The two had been staring at each other, waiting for the one to make the first move. In the midst of their stalemate, Olivia attempted to call out to them.

"Afomia?"

However, there was no answer. The Templar Knight had only one goal in mind, eliminating all those who opposed the light. Eventually, both sides lost their patience, and the battle began.

Olivia watched as her two friends clashed against one another. One possessed the power of light and the other, the power of darkness. It represented an eternal struggle that has continued since the beginning of time. However, for Olivia, she had difficulty processing what her friends had become.

"Saanjh... Afomia..." She choked back.

"Looks like we made it in time." Ehsaas said as he slowly limped his way to the Summoner.

"Ehsaas! What happened to Afomia? She didn't respond to me at all. It's as if she doesn't know who I am!"

"She has achieved the status of a Holy Templar knight. However, in doing so, she had to sacrifice everything that bound her to the physical world. All her emotions and memories are gone."

"No... They shouldn't be fighting like this. We have to help them!" Olivia cried.

"What can we do? Both their powers have far exceeded our limits."

"Ehsaas! This isn't like you. You always have a plan."

"I'm sorry, not this time." He sounded defeated.

Afomia's radiant spear landed a hit against the Chaos Mage. The previous battles were starting to have an effect on Saanjh's body. The Holy Templar could sense this was her opportunity to strike.

"Begone foul beast!" She called out.

The spear was overflowing with radiant light energy. The transcendent Templar was about to drive the weapon into her enemy but something within Saanjh began to resonate.

Standing behind Saanjh was a large chaos avatar pulsing with negative magical energy. The Holy Templar knew her current power would not be enough to stop her enemy. In order to balance the playing field, the Templar put her hands together and a giant made of light energy stood above Afomia.

There was a small moment of silence until the chaos avatar beated its chest and let out a beastly warcry. The giant of light was not intimidated. In fact, it provoked its adversary further.

After a lengthy staredown, Saanjh made the first move. The chaos avatar emulated every single one of Saanjh's movements. Similarly, the being of light worked the same for Afomia.

The chaos titan threw a punch at its archnemesis, but the light giant deflected it away with its palm. Afomia then motioned her hands and began furiously attacking with both her palms. This caused the being of light to suddenly grow multiple arms. With all those extra hands, the light avatar unleashed a fury of palms in rapid succession. In contrast, the chaos avatar had only two arms to defend itself. It would block one palm only to be struck by five others.

After taking multiple strikes, Saanjh and her avatar were still standing. Despite taking all that damage, the chaos giant let out another warcry, and now it was enraged. Saanjh commanded it by throwing a punch from the front. Afomia was ready to block, thinking it was just a routine attack. However, when the chaos titan swung its arm, its limb suddenly disappeared into a rift.

The Templar was confused and now had her guard down. Then, appearing on the Light Titan's blind side, another rift appeared, and out if it was the fist of the chaos giant striking the light titan right in the head.

The chaos avatar delivered a few more hits in a similar way until the being of light created a barrier to halt its enemy's assault. Saanjh and Afomia were both using the short break to regain some of their energy. They were still breathing heavily, but not wanting to give the other an advantage, they continued to battle.

FROM A DISTANCE, OLIVIA and Ehsaas continued to watch. It was difficult for the two, especially Olivia. With each hit the two titans landed against one another, felt as if a sword were piercing her heart.

"Ehsaas, I can't bear to watch this any longer!"

"I know how you feel, but there is nothing we can do." He replied sadly.

"Ugh! Fine! If you aren't going to do anything, then just stay here and watch!" She stormed off.

"Wait, what are you... Olivia, stop!" Ehsaas called after her.

The Summoner had left the Detective in her dust. She ran toward the two colossal combatants, who continued to trade hits against each other. Regardless of the cataclysm they were causing, Olivia tried to help her friends.

"Afomia! Saanjh! Stop fighting!" She screamed up at them; they ignored her and fought on.

Nevertheless, Olivia didn't give up as she continued to move closer, hoping her voice would eventually reach them. Once again, the Summoner called out for Afomia and Saanjh, but in the midst of doing so, Olivia got caught by the collateral damage when both avatars clashed with a powerful swing. The two titans shrugged off the hit and were ready to fight again. In contrast, lying on the ground below them was Olivia, unconscious.

It was at this moment, where both Afomia and Saanjh saw Olivia and felt a massive backlash in their bodies. They both felt a surge of pain in their heads as they began to seize up. The energies in their bodies could no longer be contained and were being released. Slowly, they grew weaker, until they could no longer sustain the powers of the avatars. The colossal figures crumbled and the two girls were descending rapidly to the ground.

Ehsaas was quick and managed to grab Saanjh before the impact. However, that left Afomia in danger as the Detective had his hands full. He immediately turned to where he thought he would find her. Thankfully, someone had caught her. It was Arianna, who casted a levitation spell to prevent Afomia from sustaining any additional injuries.

The Support Mage was still weak from earlier, but she managed to hold the spell for a little longer before letting Afomia lay gently on the ground. Once she landed safely, Ehsaas arrived, carrying Saanjh over his shoulder.

"Thank you for saving her." Ehsaas expressed his gratitude.

"Any friend of Saanjh, is a friend of mine." She smiled weakly.

Ehsaas put Saanjh down to rest comfortably against a tree. He pulled out a container of water that he had kept on his sash.

"Here, have some." He offered it to Arianna.

"Thanks, but you should save it for everyone else. Don't waste that on me." Arianna said, looking away.

"Don't say that. Everyone is important." Ehsaas said firmly.

"No it's not that. The longer I'm alive, the more he will abuse my powers."

"He? You mean..."

Before Ehsaas could say the name, a small portal opened and out walked the Necromancer, Bal.

This was the Archer's first up close encounter with the nefarious magician and Ehsaas could feel his enemy's presence. It was difficult just to stand near his aura. Although Ehsaas was able to stop his body from shaking, he knew nothing in his arsenal could defeat such an opponent. He could only wait and watch, hoping nothing would happen to his friends.

Thinking so little of the Detective, Bal walked past Ehsaas. He then continued forward until he saw both Afomia and Saanjh's body, lying unconscious on the ground.

"Well, well, she was able to hold her ground against a holy templar. Her potential might be greater than I even imagined." He said more to himself.

"You're despicable." Arianna directed her comment at Bal.

"Oh? How so? I spared both your lives, didn't I?"

"You pit two friends against each other, and watch the fight for your amusement."

"Tch. The Templar turning into a transcendent being was not something I anticipated. However, it worked in my favour. I know for certain this girl has the power to bring glory back to the mages!" He was excited for a moment, but turned to face Arianna with a demand. "Now, heal her."

Arianna looked at Saanjh and saw the terrible condition she was in. "No, I will not allow Saanjh to go through that dreadful experience again."

"Wrong answer." Bal was furious and ready to punish Arianna but an arrow was fired right at his forehead. The Necromancer casted a spell without much hesitation to block the attack. He turned to find Ehsaas holding the crossbow in his direction.

"Next one will actually hit your head." Ehsaas threatened the mage, while taking aim.

Without hesitation, Bal teleported in front of the Archer and placed his own head in front of the crossbow, daring the Archer to let his arrow fly. "Go ahead. I'll give you this one shot."

Ehsaas had his finger near the trigger but he couldn't pull it. He put down his crossbow and hung his head down in defeat. "I know you are immortal. My shot wouldn't have done anything to you."

"A wise choice. Perhaps I will consider sparring your life."

"I just have one question." Ehsaas had an urgent question.

"Hm?"

"Of all the magic you could have chosen to master through your immortal life span, why did you pick necromancy?"

The Mage took a few steps and took a moment of silence before replying to Ehsaas. "Tell me, what is something humans desire but is ever so fleeting?"

"Is this a trick question? You just gave me the answer. Immortality." Ehsaas answered with stern confidence.

"My, my, you are indeed a detective. But I didn't need necromancy for that."

Ehsaas wasn't in the mood for riddles but seeing as this was the best way to stall, he played along. He thought for a moment and wondered what Bal desired that could be achieved through necromancy.

"Well, I'm going to take a wild guess and say since you don't seem to have many friends, perhaps friendship is the answer?" The Archer replied sarcastically.

"Oh, so close." Bal responded equally sarcastically.

"So what is it?"

"Loyalty."

"Loyalty? What would you need..." Ehsaas was puzzled by the answer.

Suddenly, Bal's eyes began to turn dark red. He was casting a powerful spell that shook the earth. Ehsaas was doing his best to maintain his balance, while cracks began to form on the ground. From below, skeletal arms began to reach out. Crawling out from the depths was an army of skeletal mages that Bal had summoned.

"Are those...?" Ehsaas was nervous about the answer.

"Yes, they are the mages that did not agree with his plan." Arianna was the one who answered.

Ehsaas was in shock by what he was seeing and what he had heard. "Is that what you plan to do with Saanjh?"

"Your friend has proven her usefulness. She has far exceeded my expectations. At this rate, she could even surpass my power."

"And what about her?" Ehsaas was referring to Arianna.

"I have found that the Support Mage's healing abilities could be very useful. However, if she continues to disobey, then her fate will be the same as those who oppose me."

"Why are you doing all this?" Ehsaas asked.

"Those filthy creatures destroyed my brethren. I had to watch as they all fell one by one, while only a few of us survived. I've had to live with those memories constantly in my head for all this time. Then there are those insolent humans who ostracized us. They had forgotten who were the ones that fought for their freedoms. They too, shall pay." Bal made a fist as he was seething in anger.

"I can't imagine what it must be like to have the burden of those feelings. But I know someone who's been through a similar situation to you. However, he is nothing like you, I think immortality has gotten to your head." Ehsaas was referring to Rice.

"Tch, and I thought you would be different from the others. How foolish of me." The Necromancer sounded a bit disappointed.

Tired of their conversation, Ehsaas fired a preemptive shot hoping to catch Bal off guard. To the Archer's dismay, his arrow was split in half. Bal's eyes were glowing, and swirling around him was a storm of bones. Using some of the skeletal debris around him, Bal launched a flurry of bone shards at the Detective.

Ehsaas had nothing to defend himself except his arms. He braced himself expecting the worst, but casting a barrier to protect him was Arianna. Seeing her defiance, Bal redirected his attack towards the Support Mage. She was able to create a small shield but some of the shards pierced through and cut her arms.

Bal had victory within his grasp but rolling towards his feet were multiple round pebbles. They exploded around him and created a smoke screen, which was amplified by his own bonestorm. The Necromancer had to halt his spell to clear the smoke from his sight. When his vision had returned, both the Support Mage and the Detective had disappeared.

Chapter 21: Turn of the Tide

Hiding in a bush, Ehsaas was hatching a plan to defeat Bal. "Think you can do it?" He asked.

"You really think we have a chance?" Arianna questioned.

"Slim, but it ain't zero." Ehsaas continued to hope.

After giving his reply, they could both hear footsteps around their vicinity. The Necromancer was near and they couldn't hide for much longer. Ehsaas and Arianna looked at each other, knowing what they had to do.

Popping out of the bushes was Ehsaas firing an arrow at his target. Without much movement, a skeletal arm appeared from the ground and caught the arrow.

Bal then began to cast plasma skulls that locked on to their target. Ehsaas reacted by manoeuvring through the forest, forcing some of the plasma skulls to collide with the trees. However, some of the projectiles could not be eluded but thankfully, Arianna was able to stop them by casting a barrier for Ehsaas.

It was at this point that Bal grew tired of their nuisance. He slammed the ground, causing countless skeletal hands to rise from the ground. All the hands reached and grabbed the Detective and the Support Mage.

Both Ehsaas and Arianna were no longer able to move. Bal stood in front of the Archer and asked, "Any final words?"

"Yeah, look out for the elephant." Ehsaas said, nodding behind the Necromancer.

Bal was confused until he heard the roar of the Spirit Elephant.

"What? You are..." He was surprised that Nicholas had been summoned.

The elephant stomped his two feet, creating a shockwave that shattered all the skeleton arms that were restraining Ehsaas and Arianna.

"How are you here when your summoner is..."

Bal looked over and saw Olivia. Although she had her belly down against the ground, she was conscious, holding out Nicholas' summoning stones.

"I see, resilient aren't you?" Bal said loathingly to Olivia. Nicholas' eyes were coloured with rage. He had not forgotten their first encounter. With all his might, the elephant attempted to squish the Necromancer under his feet. However, two giant skeleton arms came up to keep the elephant's stops from crushing Bal.

The elephant and the Dark Mage were locked in a power struggle. This was the opportunity that Ehsaas was looking for. He aimed his shot with Bal's back facing him. The arrow would have nailed the target in the head, but another skeletal arm rose up, and protected the sorcerer.

Ehsaas was caught off guard realizing that might have been his last chance. Bal was enraged and he channeled that energy to unleash a deadly nova pulse that sent both Nicholas and Ehsaas slamming hard onto the ground.

The Spirit Elephant fainted and Ehsaas was barely able to move. He struggled to get up but fell back down. He could also see his enemy's footsteps before him.

"For someone with no special abilities, you have been an absolute pest." Bal spat at the boy.

"Heh, I'll take that as a compliment." Ehsaas returned a weak smile.

Aggravated by his comment, Bal casted a death grip spell that had Ehsaas suffocating. Bal was ready to fully strangle the Detective, but the Necromancer felt something stab his neck forcing him to release his grip on Ehsaas.

The Detective was dropped on the ground, gasping for air. At the same time, Bal looked around to find the one who struck him. Appearing back into sight was Arianna.

"A camouflage spell? You are full of surprises as well." Bal was somewhat impressed.

Arianna nervously shook as she braced herself to fight. Bal was about to cast a curse on her, but nothing happened. He tried again, but with the same result. He was confused as he looked at Arianna.

"What did you do to me?" He snarled.

Arianna was clueless but Bal demanded an answer.

"Anti-magic toxin." Ehsaas interrupted.

"What?" Bal wanted clarity.

"I laced an arrow designed to specifically deal with mages like you." For a moment, Bal reflected on his battle against Ehsaas. "You planned this!"

Ehsaas nodded. "I knew you would underestimate her. It's only fitting that she deals you the finishing blow."

There was a bit of silence before a laugh began to form. Bal was laughing maniacally.

"What's so funny?" Ehsaas asked.

"I'm sorry, you just spoke as if you have defeated me. Please enlighten me, which one of you will do it? The Summoner is barely conscious. Both Saanjh and your Templar Knight are defeated. That Support Mage doesn't know a single spell that can hurt me. And finally, you can't even get up."

Ehsaas knew Bal was right. No one was currently strong enough to defeat the Necromancer even though he temporarily couldn't cast his magic.

"I'm also aware of this toxin of yours. The effects should only last for about thirty minutes." He smirked.

Ehsaas tried to hide his face, but Bal was telling the truth. Without his powers, Bal resorted to ordering his minions to clean up his remaining enemies. All hope seemed lost and when things couldn't have gotten worse, a bat flew by and landed near the Necromancer.

Everyone thought it was just a normal bat, until it stopped suppressing its energy. Slowly, the bat was going through a metamorphosis and out of it emerged, the Vampire Lord.

Olivia, Ehsaas, and Arianna could feel the dreadful aura of the Count. Even Bal, who was normally calm, was visibly distressed. In contrast, the Vampire Overlord was applauding the Necromancer.

"A wonderful performance, you have really outdone yourself." He greeted everyone with a smile.

"You... What are you planning?" Bal looked at the Vampire Lord in disgust.

"Me? Why, nothing. There was no need for me to plot anything. I just let everything play itself out. And the results couldn't have been better if I had planned it."

Bal was getting nervous. He knew there was still a lot of time before his powers would return. His only hope was to strike the vampire before he could react. The Sorcerer commanded all his skeletal mages to simultaneously attack the blood monarch before he could react. The combined magical strike collided and created a massive explosion. However, when the dust cleared, the emperor of the night stood, barely damaged.

Bal was frightened by the results, which was a sight that Olivia, Ehsaas, and Arianna never thought they would see.

"Your summons could use an extra power boost. Here, let me demonstrate for you."

The Dark Tyrant made contact with two of the skeletal mages. In the process, they morphed into vampire mages that responded only to their new master. The two newly created minions completely demolished all the skeletal mages within seconds. As his minions fell, Ball saw all hope had faded away and he fell to his knees.

The Overlord walked past Bal, no longer seeing the Sorcerer as a threat. Even if the magician's powers returned, he had lost the will to fight. The vampire was making his way towards the cabin until Ehsaas spoke up.

"What did you do to him?" He was referring to Rice.

The vampire responded by throwing a piece of fabric he had torn, to the Detective. "That should answer your question."

Although Ehsaas was able to confirm the torn piece belonged to Rice, he refused to believe it.

Seeing no reason to stay, the Vampire Lord called for one of his Humbat to clean up the mess. He then made his way to where the dark portal ritual was located.

Chapter 22: Impending Doom

After its master had left, the Humbat was left to do as it pleased. It was drooling over the amount of food available. Would it choose Saanjh or Afomia, both weren't even conscious. Perhaps Ariana, who couldn't cast a spell due to exhaustion, or Ehsaas who was lying on the ground.

None of those were its choice, as it had its eyes set on Olivia. Slowly, the Humbat crawled towards its prey. Olivia was no longer able to move and neither Ehsaas nor Arianna could help her. The Summoner held tightly to her stones that were in her hand. Memories of each of her companions appeared: Saanvi, Nicholas, Sabir, Attis, and finally, Max.

The Humbat stood with its jaws wide open, ready to devour the Summoner. Its fangs were inches away from biting Olivia but a stone in her hand, that had lost its marks, was suddenly glowing again. The light diverted the Humbat's attention to the stone, which was pulsing with energy.

Slowly, a spirit animal was beginning to emerge above Olivia. As it was manifesting, Olivia could see wings beginning to spread. Although she couldn't clearly see the new companion, its presence felt very familiar.

"Max?!" Olivia felt a surge of energy.

Finally, the summoning had stabilized and manifesting with wings stretched wide open was Max's new form, a phoenix.

While Olivia, Ehsaas, and Arianna were in awe of the radiant bird, the Humbat did not share the same enthusiasm. Instead, it unleashed a deafening roar, forcing everyone to cover their ears. However, Max was not fazed. With a swoosh of both his wings, he created a fierce gale that struck the Humbat in the windpipes, silencing the creature.

Max then looked around and saw his allies: Nicholas the rhino, Saanvi and her wolves, Sabir the elephant, Ehsaas, Arianna, Saanjh, Afomia, and Olivia. Seeing their ailments, he released some of his feathers that descended down and landed on their bodies.

The feathers began to beam with energy, rejuvenating all those who made contact with it. Ehsaas and Arianna had been reinvigorated. All of Olivia's summons were able to return to their summoning stones fully healthy. Both Saanjh and Afomia were starting to wake up from their unconscious state.

"Ugh, what happened?" Afomia asked while holding her head. As she opened her eyes, she saw the destruction that had been caused to the forest. She had a glimpse in her memory from when she was in her transcendent form.

"Did I... Cause all this damage?"

Afomia was horrified by that possibility, but she snapped back to reality when she saw the Humbat recklessly stomping on the ground. Out of its frustration, it started to take flight and attempt to attack Ehsaas. The Humbat dashed through before anyone could react. The detective was in a vulnerable spot, but knocking it aside with a chaos beam was Saanjh.

The monster attempted to get up, but there was no mercy from the chaos magician. She continuously launched chaos bolts at her enemy without any remorse. Even when the Humbat had been defeated, Saanjh's fury continued. However, Olivia had enough so she appeared beside her friend and grabbed her wrist.

"That's enough."

When Olivia looked into Saanjh's eyes, there was only an ominous glow filled with hatred. However, after waiting a moment longer, Saanjh's eyes returned to normal. Her rage had subsided, and a flood of tears appeared in her eyes. Olivia embraced her friend as the Mage cried on her shoulder.

Although Saanjh didn't remember everything, she knew most of the destruction in the forest was her responsibility. As she continued to weep on Olivia's shoulder, Afomia's attention had shifted to Bal. The Templar grabbed the Sorcerer by the collar and pinned him against a tree.

"This is your fault!" Afomia yelled at the Necromancer, but he did not have a reaction. "What's wrong with you? You were awfully talkative earlier! Say something!" She demanded.

"Nothing matters anymore. We are all doomed." Bal said in despair.

That only fueled Afomia's anger. The once disciplined templar reached for her spear and held it near her enemy. "I haven't the slightest idea what you are saying, but I'm going to end this right here!"

"Go ahead, this is your chance." Bal beckoned her.

Afomia thought he was mocking her strength and she was ready to drive the spear at Bal's chest. However, Ehsaas appeared and held her weapon back.

"What are you doing?" The Templar was not pleased.

"Don't get me wrong, I can't stand the sight of him either, but he's not the problem right now."

"What do you mean?"

Afomia was confused, so Ehsaas summarized the events that took place while she was unconscious. After hearing what her friend had said, she reluctantly dropped the Necromancer to the ground.

"Don't make me regret sparring your life." Afomia threw the necromancer down.

"Tch, I'm immortal, remember? You can't kill me." Bal replied annoyingly.

"I'm going to rip you to..."

"Afomia!" Ehsaas shouted, and she begrudgingly restrained herself. Then, the Detective approached the Necromancer alone.

"You are making quite the gamble. Sparring your enemy's life, hoping he will help you defeat the greater threat." Bal knew exactly what Ehsaas was planning.

"No! You can't be serious!" Afomia reacted.

"We don't have a choice. The Vampire Lord is far too powerful. We need his help."

"There's no way I'm fighting alongside him. Not after what he has done to Saanjh." Olivia protested.

Ehsaas tried to reason with his allies but Bal interrupted. "Then allow me to put all of you at ease. I have no intention of joining forces with the likes of you lot."

The Detective was taken aback. He realized there was no way this alliance would come together. He was ready to leave without Bal, until Arianna began walking towards the Necromancer.

Everyone else watched in silence, wondering what the Mage would say. She stopped before the Necromancer and to everyone's surprise, she slapped the dark sorcerer across the face. They were all in shock as Arianna spoke.

"For so long, I was forced to watch you commit so many heinous acts. Now, you have a chance at redemption, and you choose to be a coward. To think, I used to fear you because I thought you were powerful, but now I can see you are the one who is truly scared."

"Tch tough words. Why don't you repeat them once my powers return." Bal provoked the Support Mage, but Ehsaas stepped in.

"There's no sense in wasting our energy any longer with him. We should focus on stopping the blood tyrant."

Arianna agreed and turned her back on the Necromancer. As the mage left, Afomia and Ehsaas quickly followed after her. Saanjh's tears were beginning to dry, but she never looked at Bal's face as she joined up with the others. Olivia looked back at the Necromancer with a disdainful look before heading out as well.

Left alone was Bal, who sat feeling defeated, thinking about how his plans had gone so wrong. As he was reminiscing, he could hear footsteps approaching his way. He thought it was more of the Vampire Lord's minions, but then he saw who the footsteps belong to.

"You..."

Chapter 23: End of an Era

After making his way through the entrance of the cabin, the Vampire Lord found where the ritual circle was. He ordered his two mage minions to stand at opposite ends of the circle. He held out his hand and spoke in an ancient language, causing the circle to light up dark red.

The two minions' bodies were no longer in their control as they began to levitate from the ground. In addition, their bodies began to go into a seizure as their life force was being siphoned.

Once they were sapped of all their essence, the portal began to manifest. Grotesque limbs were beginning to reach out as there were countless monsters trying to force their way out. However, the circle suddenly lost its glow and the portal was no longer opening any wider. The Dark Lord realized begrudgingly that the portal would not open fully without more sacrifices.

OUTSIDE THE CABIN, several vampiric minions stood on guard to prevent the ritual from being disrupted. There were two patrolling around the perimeter when suddenly, one of them was struck in the heart. It was a silver bolt that belonged to Ehsaas.

With the first minion dealt with, the others were alerted about the intruders' presence. A fleet of ravenous bats began rushing towards the Detective. They attempted to swarm the human only to be incinerated by a flaming gust of wind. It was the Spirit Phoenix: Max.

Seeing many of their allies burn, the rest of the minions attacked simultaneously. Olivia appeared and summoned all her companions to aid her in the fight. Ehsaas even hopped on the rhino's back and rode into battle.

As the dark forces were distracted, Afomia, Saanjh, and Arianna snuck into the cabin undetected. They made their way inside until they arrived at where the ritual circle was located.

"There it is!" Saanjh yelled.

"That's strange..." Afomia thought to herself.

"What is it?" Saanjh asked.

"The circle doesn't look active and there's no portal opened." Afomia pointed out.

"You're right. The Count should be here and the portal as well. Where is his pale face at?" Saanjh wondered out loud.

As Afomia and Saanjh were conversing, Arianna felt something was off about their situation. She looked closely at the circle and noticed a slight anomaly that many would not have seen.

"Afomia, Saanjh, we have to get out of here! It's a trap!" She called out.

However, the realization came too late. Materializing from behind Saanjh and Arianna were two dark empty coffins. Each one dragged a mage inside and became sealed once they had their captive. The coffins were then telekinetically moved into opposite ends of the circle.

When everything was in place, the reality shift spell that covered up the active portal and the ritual circle was now lifted. Afomia was horrified by the scene of seeing her friends being offered as sacrifices and attempted to stop the ritual. However, stepping out of a dark rift was the Vampire Lord, obstructing the Templar's way.

"I'm afraid I can't allow you to interfere." He said in a raspy voice.

Afomia channeled as much of her holy energy into her spear before thrusting it at her enemy. With just the palm of his right hand, the Count was able to block the Templar's strike. Afomia attempted to push through but the Vampire Lord sent Afomia slamming to the ground.

As she looked up, she saw Saanjh and Arianna's life force being drained as they were trapped inside the coffins. As a result, the opening of the portal was slightly increasing. Seeing this, Afomia tried to pick up her spear but her strength was failing her. Watching her struggle, the Blood Tyrant walked to the Templar, attempting to convert her.

"You will make a fine soldier of the undead." He reached out his hand to her.

"I'd rather be buried alive than serve you." She replied in disgust.

"Heh, you won't have much choice." He said as he was about to place his fangs on Afomia's neck, but obstructing him was a bone wall that manifested between him and the Templar. Once they were separated, a fire ball struck the tyrant's back and he felt a burning pain that took some of his regenerative powers to heal. When his wound healed, he looked behind and found who was responsible.

"You two..." He snarled.

Standing in defiance of the dark master were two magicians that were averse to him many centuries ago, Rice and Bal. The Necromancer's powers had returned, but more importantly, his will to fight was rejuvenated.

The Overlord began to have flashbacks about that battle. The images of defeat still haunted him, causing him to become enraged. He released a loud bellow before transforming into his primal form. His figure looked completely devoid of any qualities. He was an amalgamation of all the monsters he had devoured. Without hesitation, the grotesque aberration ran at the two magicians.

Afomia couldn't believe the turn of events but she could not rest now. With hope restored, she was able to gather herself to stand up. However, it was a struggle for her to move towards the portal. She was about to stumble but she was caught by one of her friends.

"Ehsaas!" She cried.

"I'll help get you to Saanjh, you'll do the rest." With Afomia's arm over his shoulder, Ehsaas assisted the Templar towards the dark coffin.

"What about Arianna?" Afomia questioned.

"Olivia has that covered." They looked at the opposite end of the battle field and saw Olivia standing by the other coffin.

When Afomia was standing before one of the dark coffins, she gave a look over to Olivia and they knew what they had to do. In unison, the Holy Knight and the Summoner channeled their remaining power to create an armour for themselves. Afomia was encased in holy armour while Olivia had on spirit armour.

With all her might, Afomia swung her holy spear at the coffin. On the opposite end, Olivia had giant spirit animal claws appear on her hands and she slashed the coffin with ferocity. As they struck the coffins, recoil of dark energy began to strike their bodies. Thankfully, the armour they casted on themselves helped shield them from taking the damage.

Eventually, they both shattered the coffin, but the energy backlash sent Olivia and Afomia landing on their backs. Their armours had disappeared and nearly all their energy was gone, but their mission had been accomplished. The two mages, Arianna and Saanjh were freed from their prison.

It took her a moment, but Saanjh managed to get up on her own. She looked to find Arianna and Ehsaas near her. The next thing that caught Saanjh's attention were her two friends lying on the ground.

"Olivia! Afomia!" Saanjh cried.

"They will be alright. They are just resting." Ehsaas' response put Saanjh at ease, until Arianna noticed the portal.

"Oh no, the portal is getting larger." Arianna sounded frightened.

"We have to close it now before it's too late." Saanjh said with urgency.

"Not yet, I have a plan, but I need both of your help to make it work." Ehsaas said.

"Okay, tell us what we need to do." Arianna replied.

The battle between the elite combatants raged on. Although the primal vampire's power was unparalleled, the combined efforts of the mages were currently keeping the Tyrant at bay.

Bal created multiple bone lances and hurled them at the hulking monstrosity. Being such a large target, most of the lances hit its mark but the fiend shrugged it off and continued its rampage.

Rice attempted multiple elemental attacks. He first froze the limb of the savage creature and then landed a meteor spell to follow up. The combination of spells shattered one of the abomination's limbs, only to have it regenerate another arm to take its place.

"I can't believe he's even stronger than the last time we fought him." Bal was breathing heavily.

"I mean, he does have all the time in the world to practice." Rice replied.

"Tch, couldn't he have found better use of his time instead of plotting his revenge?"

"Ha! You're the one to talk." Laughed Rice.

The vampiric amalgamation was disgusted by their bantering. It unleashes a corrosive sludge from its mouth at the two pests. Rice created an ice wall that successfully nullified the attack, but he wasn't expecting the follow up strike. Tentacles grew from the monstrosity's back and he swung one of them at the vulnerable mage.

"Look out!" Bal shouted.

Bal jumped behind Rice and was slashed by the tentacle. It was laced with venom that paralyzed the Necromancer causing him excruciating pain.

The enemy would not let up as it launched the rest of the tentacles. Rice could have dodged the attacks, but with his ally unable to defend himself, he stood on to face the onslaught. He slammed his hands on the ground and some of the earth beneath him rose to create a forcefield around him and Bal. Although the shield was effectively protecting the mages for the time being, it was only a matter of time before the enemy's relentless assault would break through.

As the tentacles kept slamming against the veil, the Tyrant continued towards them with a malicious smirk.

"You are quite the resilient mage. I thought I got rid of you in our earlier battle. Tell me, how did you do it?"

"Haven't you heard? A magician never reveals his secrets." He smiled.

"Then you shall perish with it!" The enemy screamed in rage. He had focused a majority of his dark energy into his fist, which decimated the barrier. With the mages now defenseless, he raised his other arm and slashed the two mages with his deadly sharp claws.

"No!" Arianna and Saanjh both uttered in despair. They couldn't believe what they were witnessing; the two lifeless bodies lying on the ground. They were in so much shock, they were unable to move and the Overlord made his way to claim the remaining mages in order to finish opening the portal.

However, the fiend was forced to halt its advancement when it noticed an arrow spiralling towards his eye. One of his tentacles caught the bolt, long before it could even touch his pupil. He searched around to find Ehsaas holding his crossbow aimed at the vampire's face.

"Tch, and what are you going to do? You are just a human with nothing but sticks and tricks. What could you possibly do to me?" The Vampire Lord scoffed.

"You want to find out?" Ehsaas' comment made the Count laugh hysterically.

"Insolent worm. What kind of fool do you take me for?"

"One that talks too much."

The Vampire Lord was infuriated by Ehsaas' presence. He was ready to tear the Detective to shreds but then was suddenly struck by a fusion blast that pushed him towards the portal.

"What?! How are you two still alive?!" The Vampire Lord saw both Rice and Bal still in fighting condition.

"I didn't think you would fall for my clone ability twice. I mean, that's how I got away from you last time." Rice explained.

"But the..the corpses..." The enemy stuttered.

"You have no idea how difficult it was to conjure two bodies that resembled us." Bal interjected.

In addition to everything, the Count didn't notice that Arianna casted a camouflage spell on both Bal and Rice. That allowed them to move to opposite ends of the ritual circle undetected and donate some of their powers to open the portal large enough to send the Vampire Lord back to the realm he belonged.

"No! I refuse to spend another second in that wretched place!" The Tyrant was agonizing over the thought.

His rage led to an outburst of dormant energy that further empowered him. With the extra strength boost, he was able to push back the fusion beam with his own dark energy cannon.

"If you are holding anything back, now would be a fantastic time to use it." Rice notified Bal.

"I'm afraid this is all I've got. Giving up some of our energy to open that portal is really not helping..." Bal's strength was faltering quicker than Rice's. "I'm sorry, I don't think I will last." Bal said weakly.

Suddenly, He felt a punch hit him in the face. "Hey! Are you crazy?!"

"If you have energy to get mad at me, then you definitely have more than enough to beat this unholy fiend." Rice pointed out.

"Heh, I hate it when you are right. Alright, let's do this."

They both stopped channeling the fusion beam and rolled away from each other. Then, they rushed towards the undead Overlord and tackled him together. Their combined force pushed the Tyrant towards the portal.

"Fools, without your magic, you are powerless. You can't defeat me!"

"We can't, but she can!" They yelled together.

Rice's comment made the Fiend look further past him. He saw Saanjh, who had focused all her magical energy and was unleashing her most powerful chaos wave. The spell struck Bal, Rice, and the grotesque beast simultaneously, pushing them all towards the portal.

It looked to be successful until they were forced to the entrance of the opening. The Vampire Lord desperately grabbed the edge, holding on until Saanjh's endurance would fail.

"Nice try, but you are still not good enough to..."

He was cut off as Saanjh had a sudden spike in power and began pushing him further into the portal.

"How? You shouldn't be able to..." He looked and standing behind Saanjh was Arianna, using her support abilities to increase Saanjh's strength.

Bal also witnessed this as he was getting pushed into the abyss. What he saw was the two mages working together to defeat a tyrannical force of evil. It reminded him of the era when mages were at their brightest.

"What are you thinking about?" Rice asked.

"The future of the mages will be in good hands." Bal replied with a tear rolling down his eyes.

"They will lead them well." Rice wasn't just referring to Saanjh and Arianna, but to Ehsaas Olivia, and Afomia as well.

Bal nodded. "Let's finish this."

Rice and Bal gave one final push together. Arianna stacked one last empowerment spell on Saanjh, allowing her to give one final outburst into her chaos blast.

The combined strength of everyone was too much for the nefarious Overlord to overcome. He was forced further into the portal and plunged into the void. In contrast, both Rice and Bal's essence began to scatter into the air. The immortal curse that binded them had been lifted as Saanjh's attack dealt the finishing blow.

Epilogue

Approximately one year after the threat of the oppressive Vampire Lord had been abolished, peace had been restored to Diamondvania. Suspicion amongst the villagers took some time to eliminate. But thanks to Arianna's newly discovered ability, she was able to dispel those who had the werewolf or vampire curse. Arianna spent much of her time in Diamondvania as the town's trusted healer.

Moreover, Saanjh started her own training academy for mages. She helped magicians of all ages learn to control and use their talents to help the town prosper. She was challenged by many of her students, none of whom could best her in a duel.

Ehsaas was hired by Mayor Corrin to become Head of Security in Diamondvania. He played a vital role in creating a police force to protect the villagers. There was no case that was too difficult for him to solve.

Afomia returned back to the temple where her family happily celebrated her return. Master Ruthar spoke with the elders and they were all in agreement to bestow the official title of 'Holy Knight' on her. Even after achieving that status, she continued training to hone her skills. She also taught her people to be cautious about achieving their transcendent form as she knew the heavy cost that came with such power.

Olivia roamed the wild lands around the world, where she found new companions on her journey. Together they explored the vast world and helped maintain order wherever they travelled.

All the accounts of this tale were kept in the archives of Diamondvania. This was done to ensure that the villagers would never forget the sacrifices made to restore peace to their home.

.

www.ingramcontent.com/pod-product-compliance
Lightning Source LLC
Chambersburg PA
CBHW020654180626
46816CB00003B/1282